Night-Mantled

The Best of Wily Writers

Volume One

ISBN-10: 098318240X
ISBN-13: 978-0-9831824-0-5 (Wily Writers)

DEDICATION

I'm a lucky woman. I have more loving friends than anyone should be allowed in one lifetime, and my family is a constant joy to me. I couldn't possibly name all the people who have supported me throughout the development and growth of the Wily Writers project, nor could I single out any one individual, so I'll just take a moment to toss a blanket of love out to all of you who contributed in some way to the site. Thank you for your time, your encouragement, your knowledge, your wisdom, your generosity, your talent, your tweets, and your love. Quite sincerely, I could not have done it without you.

— Angel Leigh McCoy, head editor, Wily Writers

Special Thanks

An extra dose of gratitude goes out to Dan Cole, Reagan Wright, and A.J. Thompson. Dan is the talented photographer who took our cover photo. Reagan is our model as well as one of two amazing graphic artists who perfected the image and layout for us. A.J. is the other great talent who did the lion's share of the layout for the cover.

Please check out their websites:

- Dan Cole: www.gritbox.com
- Reagan Wright: www.bluebearstudio.com
- A.J. Thompson: www.azraelarts.com

CONTENTS

"The Minimart, the Ruger, and the Girl"

by Mark W. Worthen

Come live with me and be my love
And we will some new pleasures prove…
—John Donne

Nothing really worth telling about happened on my shift that night, unless you count the dead body I found behind the minimart. It happened a little before I went home.

I was still behind the counter when the gawky morning kid showed up an hour early for his shift, and stood over me, waiting for me to move. He had me in height by about a foot, and looked like someone had shotgunned him with a load of freckles. When he walked, his strides were too long, resulting in a side-to-side motion that made me think of land-roving metronomes.

"You're not supposed to be in for another hour," I told him.

"Can't sleep, sir."

"Nick," I interrupted him. "My stepdad was 'sir,' but he liked to get drunk and beat up his family. 'Sir' is for army officers and old men." I said it over my shoulder.

Metronome Kid took my place behind the counter, and I went out the back towards the house. I couldn't see very well in the dark, and missed the damn path, ending up wandering through knee-high alfalfa.

About halfway to the house, after banging my feet and barking my shins against the piles and mounds of old junk camouflaged by the tall weeds, I kicked into something soft and heavy that nearly tumbled me into a heap of ancient and rusty rebar. The object I'd tripped over seemed softer than the rest of the angular crap in the yard. So I reached down to find out what it was, and as soon as I touched it, I knew what I'd found.

I tripped and stumbled back to the store to get a flashlight, not telling the kid anything, and returned to the body.

That's what it was, all right. A body. In the glare of the light, I saw the Hispanic kid I'd scared away from the store my first night on the job. He'd bled to death—someone had garroted him, then torn open the side of his throat and emptied him.

Oh, lucky me. No mistaking that.

Number thirteen.

♦ When the wizened old geezer got into a '69 VW Beetle with cracking yellow paint and a broken bumper, I suspected I'd been royally had. He wanted me to take this job on a permanent basis, and now that I'd signed the papers, there wasn't a damned thing I could do about it.

He cracked a frightening smile of blackened teeth and soft gums, and muttered, "I'm going to Florida, dammit," in his sandpaper-on-chalkboard voice.

"I've worked this store or one like it for upside of sixty-five years, and if I have to do it one more day, I'm going to croak. As old as I am, I'll be lucky if I actually make it to Florida. Managing to get back would be a miracle. Roger that?"

I nodded.

"She's all yours. Have at."

With that, he shook my hand through the open window of the car, thrust a ring of keys at me, and shifted into first to rumble off towards the freeway.

As I stood there, watching the dissipating cloud of dust that marked his wake, it occurred to me: he'd left me no way to get in touch with him. I looked at the jingling keys on the old-fashioned ring. I was completely on my own. I shrugged and headed inside.

Wouldn't be the first time.

♦ Transporting a corpse on a Harley is not the easiest thing in the world. Normally I'd just leave him where I found him, but factor in a dead body on property I was responsible to go with the witnesses to say I'd threatened him with a handgun the size of Cleveland, and...well, you do the math. I wouldn't stand a chance in hell.

I wanted to wait until after midnight the next evening, but with me in charge of the minimart, it would look suspicious if I had to get someone to take my shift, so I wheeled my hog back to where I'd found the kid. Heaving him onto the seat was the work of two minutes. I used a belt I'd found in the house to lash him to my back, and off we went. I had to take special care around the corners.

All of this just before sunrise. I was going to be able to get him out of *here* before daylight, but not all the way to where I wanted to leave him. The next two hours were going to be touch-and-go. If I got stopped...

I stuck to country roads. I motored up one of the canyons, all the way through Heber and around to Park City, then buried him in as deep a grave as I could manage in one of the side canyons—hunters would find him eventually, but hopefully not before the carnivorous population did.

When I'd turned the last bit of dirt to cover him, I slid off the bandana holding back my curly black hair and offered a quick and dirty prayer before leaving. It was the best I could do.

Just my luck our local serial killer would choose my freaking backyard to leave one of his vics in. With me the new guy in town, too, and a retired biker to boot. Everyone would suspect me just on general principle.

"The Vampire," as the Salt Lake Tribune dubbed him, struck eleven times between the city of Ogden and the town of Spanish Fork, all in a period of about ninety days. Lehi, where the minimart sat, fell neatly into that line. The sun was well overhead by the time I got back home and fell into bed.

I slept till my shift started and, believe it or not, I forgot about the body until several days later.

♦ So after he introduced me to the freckle-showered kid that constituted the morning shift, the old man showed me the counter, the register, the freezer, and a couple of other things I'd need to know as manager. The place looked okay, but had a broken-down quality to it—the shelves and display stands needed painting, scratches and haze marred the glass of the counter, and the windows hadn't been washed in God only knew how long. This minimart must have been around in one form or another almost as long as the old man.

"You're going to have to live up here, Sonny Jim." His voice creaked like an old wooden door in the summertime. "I don't like commuters. That going to be a problem?"

Problem? Everything in the world I gave a damn about was parked out front, in the saddlebags of my hog. I'd ditched my rented single-wide in Provo that morning.

"No...sir." The word came slowly—I had to dust it off a little before I used it. "No problem."

"Good. I've got a place out back you can use. Rent free."

Rent free? Two words I always enjoyed hearing together.

"Sounds good."

Until I actually saw the place. And I thought I was a slob.

I'd seen places like it before, the archetypical example of an aged rural Utah house gone to seed. Old junk made the lot into the graveyard of farmhouse implements: a rusted-out pickup of indistinguishable origin up on blocks, looking like it hadn't moved for decades; an old avocado-colored refrigerator with the door gone, something that might originally have been a tent trailer, an antique hulk of a sewing machine in its wooden cabinet, missing a flywheel and several other major parts, a 1950's Hotpoint stove, a tractor—I think it was a tractor—and a pile of smaller objects, looking like it'd been dumped off the back of a flatbed: rusty coffee cans, unusable tools, and piles of unidentifiable stuff elderly men can't or won't bring themselves to throw away.

All covered with clotted dust and overgrown with alfalfa.

His broken-door voice came at me again. "All the daytime people are local kids. The freckle-faced one you met today is assistant manager—he makes the schedules and so forth, but don't let him touch the money, if you're smart."

He spat in the dirt between an old generator and a clump of tall weeds. "You'll be the night man. You'll also need to be available during the day to handle problems and so forth, so stay near the phone."

Like I was going to live my life like that, but I didn't bother to mention it. Let the old geezer enjoy his vacation.

"You'll basically be me while I'm gone," he went on.

"And how long will you be gone?"

He smiled and turned back to the narrow dirt track leading through the scrap labyrinth to the front door, and let us in. Apparently the place had sat a long time. Caked with dust everywhere except, of course, the television and the sofa, the place reeked of the elderly and unwashed. Only the places where he had to walk weren't stacked with old memories or old debris.

We waded through the piles, and down a little hallway running off the main room, parallel to it. At one end of it was "my room," the only place in the house relatively free of rubbish, though the ubiquitous dust settled everywhere. I'd take care of that later if it bothered me enough.

"You can have free run of the house and kitchen," he croaked. "There's a little extra in it if you'll straighten the place up."

I'll need a bulldozer, I thought uncharitably.

"What kinds of stuff should I throw away?"

"Huh," he replied. "Any damn thing you want. Something looks interesting to you, keep it."

He pointed to the other end of the hallway. "Past the bathroom there is my room."

A pair of double doors stood at the end of the hallway, a heavy padlock holding them up. If I really wanted to, I could kick my way in, but why would I want to? To see the rest of his more personal crap? Stacks of well thumbed porn magazines? Whips and chains? Bluebeard's dead wives?

I must have stared at the door a beat too long, because he said, "I'd appreciate it if you stayed out of there."

He never did ask me for references.

If he had, I'd have given him the name of an owner of a small software company where I'd worked as a security guard, and the next-door neighbor who'd been trying for the year I'd been living in Utah to get me to join his church.

I wouldn't have given him the name of the dead general store attendant in Boise I'd had to shoot to keep him from braining me with a baseball bat, or the motorist in Phoenix who followed me for three miles when I cut him off in traffic. He'd narrowly escaped dying, but only because I'd ridden all day and was tired. When I open-handed his nose, I lost my balance and broke his cheekbone instead.

It was enough to make him stop trying to kill me.

The old man and I went back to the store, and he gave me a list of stuff to order during the next couple of weeks, the names and numbers of the day kids, the fire station, and the cops. He also gave me a check for my first month.

"I've made arrangements for you to get the rest on a monthly basis, if everything's in order."

Made arrangements. If everything's in order. Very weird.

♦ Like I said, my first night, I had to threaten the now-dead Latino kid to get him to leave the store.

Along about twelve-thirty, well into the dead hours for Lehi, an orange pickup pulled into the parking lot, an older model with wheel skirts puffed out from the bed and lots of noise coming from the cab.

Teenagers. Rowdy teenagers, probably local, most certainly drunk.

Coincidentally, a red and primer-grey Firebird that might have been a nice car once chugged in and came to a halt on the other side of the six-slot parking area. A tall, Hispanic-looking guy got out, accompanied by a blast of salsa music from antiquated, blown-out speakers. *Migrantes*—travelling to where the work is— the locals, mostly white folks with money, consider themselves somehow superior to them.

Trouble waiting to happen.

I wasn't *too* worried. I'm pretty big and scary when I need to be. Imagine the guys you've seen in the biker mags, and you've got a fair idea, although I looked a little more clean cut since I'd taken off the Jerry Garcia beard and tied my longish hair back, but I still couldn't be described as "conservative." People usually didn't want to mess with me too much.

Still, no sense being *too* trusting.

I grabbed my Ruger revolver from where I'd hidden it below the register and checked the loads, then gingerly slid it down the back of my pants and adjusted my cotton shirt to cover it.

Both parties wanted beer. Utah doesn't permit sales of more powerful alcoholic beverages unless the place is licensed as a state liquor store. This place wasn't, so beer they got. I carded them; the pickup kid's driver's license said he was twenty-two, and the Hispanic's work permit gave him twenty-four. Neither looked it. They got their 24-pack, each eying the other like two tigers circling a cage, and went out to the lot with their friends.

I smelled trouble rippling off these guys like heat patterns in the sunlight, so I propped open the door and listened. The leader of the *migrantes* didn't speak too much English, but that didn't matter. The local boys knew enough insults in Spanish to get things going. I heard words like *pendejo* and *hijo de puta* and knew there would be fighting, so I walked over to the front windows.

As I expected, one of the local kids and the *migrante* leader faced off out by the pumps. One had a switchblade and the other a nasty-looking hunting knife. I moved into the doorway to watch the proceedings.

I'd about decided to let them work it out by themselves, and dump the loser in a field I'd passed a couple of miles away, when I happened to glance over at the Firebird, then at the truck. One or two people stood at each vehicle, cheering the two fighters to greater violence. What concerned me was the full gun rack in the back window of the pickup. Knives are one thing; guns are noisy and attract unwanted attention.

I decided to handle the situation myself.

I moved out of the doorway and into the lot.

"Gentlemen," I called, using what I referred to as "the voice"—a loud tone I can put an edge to, cold and hard as a shard of ice. "You will take your fighting elsewhere. Now."

The white kid just looked at me. The Hispanic looked at one of his buddies who translated my words, then turned back to me and snarled, *"Piensas tu que puedes hacernos ir de aqui, pendejo?"*

His buddy shouted translation in a thickly accented English, "You think you can make us leave, asshole?"

Great.

I walked over to the pumps, keeping one hand near the Ruger.

"Sure do." I nodded, allowing for the language difference.

I guess this didn't need translation, because the Hispanic leader held up his hand to the local kid, fist closed, thumb and pinky extended, and shook it. *Hang loose,* the very American gesture said, and he turned the switchblade towards me.

Time to get out the cavalry. I pulled out the Ruger, thumbing the hammer back it for effect, even though I didn't need to, and aimed it at his head.

"Don't even think it," I growled. I'd been edging closer and stood about twenty feet away from him by now.

No way he could reach me alive.

The Mexican hesitated. Either he could see in my eyes I don't get out the gun unless I'm ready to use it, or he was just chicken shit. Without taking his eyes from mine, he gestured his friends into the car. Still watching me, he joined them and drove away.

I turned to the local.

"What about you?"

Everything about the kid shouted "hunter." The gun rack, the pickup. He wore a flannel shirt and bright orange NRA baseball cap. He just stood there, feet apart, staring at me. Though it was a cool evening, sweat glistened on his forehead. He was afraid, but he wasn't going to give me the satisfaction.

I wished to God he'd move, one way or the other, but no. I glanced back towards the pickup to see if anyone had gone for the rifles in the truck. Not yet; probably hadn't occurred to them they had me in firepower.

Okay, I thought, enough crap. I uncocked the gun, reversing it in my hand as I moved. Before he realized what I had in mind, I'd brought the butt down hard on his head.

As he crumpled, I said to one of his friends, "Get him out of here. I've got a long memory, and if I ever see either of you here again, you'll wish I'd shot you today."

The other boy nodded, his Adam's apple making a long, slow trip down to his collar and back. He bent and dragged the unconscious kid into the truck. I stood and watched until it sped off into the distance.

Nothing else happened that night, and I knocked off at six a.m. when the first of the daytime people showed up.

♦ I don't know if the old man counted on me bringing a weapon to the party or not, but no way was I going to work nights in a convenience store without one, especially with The Vampire stalking the streets. I felt relatively certain I could handle him, but there's a special confidence that comes from having a loaded .357 nearby.

But not too much happened the second night. Lots of customers. Kids coming in to play the video games, teenagers trying to buy beer and cigarettes, motorists wanting coffee or Pepsi to stay awake, the usual run of convenience store patrons.

The one highlight of the evening came in the form of a very pretty girl. She bought a pack of Virginia Slims and a Zippo lighter. While I rang her up, she inclined her head and looked up at me through thick, dark lashes with a smile. Long, long, straight blonde hair rested on her shoulders, one of which had been laid bare by the edge of a torn sweatshirt that said, "Hard Rock Cafe Las Vegas."

"You're new here," she said.

"Here, yeah," I replied. I've never been good with women. Witty conversation always seemed too much like work. "Not to the area, though."

"Be staying with us long?"

The urge to be straight with her overcame me—not something that happens very often. "Truthfully? No. Just long enough to fatten my bankroll."

"Yeah?" her lips stretched into a coy smile. "And where will your bankroll take you?"

I'd been trying to figure her age, but I couldn't— somewhere between seventeen and twenty-seven.

"Dunno. Denver, maybe," I replied. "Or Cheyenne. Someplace they've never—someplace I haven't been before." I was going to say, someplace where they've never heard of me or the Eliminators, but thought better of it.

Just then, a guy in jeans, a jean jacket, and a matching baseball cap walked in the door and went straight to the back of the store. He looked like a walking pile of blue denim; an empty refill mug dangled from the fingers of one hand.

She distracted me again. "I know what you mean. I'm so tired of Utah," she said. "I've been here way too long."

"I hear that," I said, rolling my eyes. "How long for you?" I'd never had such an easy time talking to a woman before. The words just tumbled out before I had to think of what to say.

She turned the package of cigarettes upside down, and tapped it into her palm, packing the tobacco.

"Six months," she said. "This time. My family lives here, so I keep coming back. I'd thought to stay this time, but it turns out I'm already tired of the place."

She slipped a cigarette out of the box and held it between full lips. In a rare display of manners, I grabbed a lighter off the rack and flicked it to life in front of her. She brushed back her hair and leaned forward to accept it, revealing a slender collarbone and an expanse of pale skin that set my pulse playing a more upbeat rhythm.

Denim Boy came up with his drink and stood behind her. She scooted over so he could pay. He swiped his Visa, signed his receipt, and left.

"So where did you come from?" I'd never have expected a pretty girl to stay so long to talk to me. It just hadn't happened before.

"Me?" I leaned forward and rested my elbows on the counter, my knee touching the Ruger. "Everywhere. Nowhere. Home is actually a little place near the Bay Area called Milpitas, but I haven't been back there in so long that I've forgotten what it was like."

Her eyes lit. "I love San Francisco. I was there once in for—well, a long time ago." A genuine smile only added to her appeal.

The conversation went on like this, about travel, likes, dislikes, backgrounds, everything, nothing, for more than an hour. And then, with a flirtatious toss of

13

her cornsilk hair and a promise to come back and see me again, she finally left.

As I watched her go, her hips swaying gently in the fluorescent light, I realized I liked her.

Her name was Lysette.

◆ My last evening on the job, sitting behind the counter, waiting for the people of Lehi to come in for their beer and chips, I helped myself to a copy of the *Provo Herald* that had been delivered earlier that night.

After finishing the crossword puzzle—well, three-quarters of it, anyway; I have never been able to finish a crossword puzzle in my life—I tossed the paper to one side. When I looked up, she was standing there again, behind a styro cup of coffee, an almost coy smile on her face.

She took her place by the side of the register, and we began talking. After a long discussion on the subject of books, music, movies, all the things you wouldn't expect a biker like me to know about, the conversation rolled around again to travel. I remembered her mentioning she'd only been in Utah for a little while, so I asked her where home was.

She got a sad little half-grin on her face, and said, "It's not really anywhere, Nick. I move around a lot. I was born in Charleston, South Carolina, but I haven't been back there for a very long time."

"You don't sound Southern at all," I said.

"Don't I?" she asked, a wistful look coming over her face. "I guess it's been long enough for me to lose most of the accent. Like I said, it's been years and years. I left there when I was a little girl. My parents took me to New York."

"City?"

She nodded. "That's right."

"And you were an only child." It wasn't a question.

"How did you know that?"

"You said they took *me* to New York, not *us*," I said, rather pleased with my deductive reasoning.

A real smile—highlighting that innocent look—lit her face. "You're a perceptive man, Nicky. Where did you learn to pay attention to the things people say?"

I looked down, a little embarrassed. "The road, I guess. You pay attention or you die."

"I know the road." She looked straight into my eyes. "It's not just that. You're a survivor."

I looked back at her, mesmerized. Her eyes were striking, beautiful and big with long lashes, though I couldn't really say what color they were. They just captured me.

"But it's not just that, either. You're different, Nick. Most survivors look out for number one. You, you're a person, not like some I meet on the road. You don't go around indiscriminately pushing people out of your way."

Still locked into those eyes, I said, "Don't be too sure about that."

"I can be sure about more than you think, Nick."

She dropped her eyes to the counter, breaking the spell that held me. "Damn. I forgot my cigarettes."

I got a pack of Slims from the rack, packed and opened them, and offered her one. She took it with a smile, and I lit it for her.

"You know," she said, "you mentioned moving on soon." Her eyes went down to the counter, then: "I like you, Nick. A lot."

I liked her a lot, too. Maybe more than a lot. I knew the routine, though; boy meets girl. Girl uses boy to get what she wants. Girl subsequently tells boy to go screw himself. And I was pretty sure she was way too young for me.

The big problem that complicated everything was the feeling that came to me when she said, "I like you." It had been a long, long time since any woman had said those words in my presence. There was a distinct possibility she was lying through her teeth. There was also the possibility that she felt that same way I did. I'd often wondered about love at first sight.

So, I figured, what the hell?

"I like you, too," I replied. "I'm leaving in two weeks. Wanna come?"

Her entire face brightened, like someone had turned on a Fresnel spotlight behind it.

"Yeah, Nicky, I do. Really."

"Just to get out of here?" I wasn't sure I'd heard right. Had she misunderstood the question?

She smiled again. Wistfully? "Let's see what happens, huh?"

Couldn't ask for more than that. "Plan on it, then."

We started talking again. She stayed till my shift ended early the next morning, and together we went back to the old fart's house. It was good. Really good. She made love with a strange combination of tenderness and violence, leaving evidence of her passion. When it was done, we fell asleep in each other's arms, and when I woke up, she was gone.

I went into the moldy kitchen and made myself a cup of coffee, and while I waited for it, I picked up the paper I'd brought back to the house with me, thinking to finish the puzzle.

This time I saw the headline. And it reminded me of the body.

"VAMPIRE" CLAIMS THIRTEENTH VICTIM

Huh. They didn't know their vic was actually the fourteenth. So with my guy, two the same week. It seemed our killer was getting "hungrier." A twenty-year-old had been strangled to death and drained of blood in the town of American Fork, behind a grocery store just a few miles down the road.

I sprinted back to the place I'd found the kid and looked around. As I expected, I found a bloody guitar string lying in the dirt near where his head had been.

I ran to the store and grabbed the Ruger from its hiding place under the counter. The kid obviously hadn't known it was there, because he stared at me with an open mouth as I popped the cylinder to make sure it was loaded.

"Bored," I said, trying to sound nonchalant. "Going to do some target practice."

"Yeah, okay," he replied, trembling as he moved away from me. He didn't look convinced; he did look scared shitless.

The Ruger was still full. I stopped by the Harley, got a handful of spare bullets, and stuffed them into my jeans pockets.

♦ Being alone in that house gave me the creepiest feeling.

I'm not a wuss, at least I've never considered myself such, but I was always thankful I went to bed at sunrise after my shift ended. Unfortunately, one Sunday, I lay down and slept like a baby—for about four hours. Then I woke up and couldn't get back to sleep. Lysette was on my mind—Lord, that must make me sound like either a lovesick moron or a country music singer. Some Sominex from the store only made me feel fuzzy, but not at all sleepy. I wandered back to the house through the living room to my dormitory.

The furniture that wasn't broken was at least forty years old, and looked as though it had never been recovered or refinished. The wallpaper was yellowed and peeling in places, the bathrooms hadn't been cleaned in at least a year, and you couldn't see out the windows for the grime.

Folded on my bed lay an age-yellowed but seemingly clean sheet, and below that, a threadbare old Army blanket. I thought once I made my bed and got it livable, things would be just a bit more homey, but if anything, the atmosphere in that house got worse.

Now don't get me wrong; I've never been superstitious. It's just that I had the oddest feeling that there was something more here than met the eye.

I shook my head to clear the garbage.

I hate insomnia.

Usually when I can't sleep, I read. I prefer the classics, believe it or not. Joseph Conrad is my favorite, but Dickens runs a close second. I'd just finished the John Dos Passos in my saddlebag, and hadn't had a chance to visit a bookstore.

So I wandered through the house looking at the interesting stuff crammed literally into every corner. You might think, "Okay, that took five minutes, what did you do the rest of the day?"

But you'd be wrong. This was the house of an old man who never threw anything away. I respected his wishes and didn't break into his bedroom, but I found a lot of stuff in the den. A big secretary-type desk there contained all kinds of pictures that held my attention for quite a while. Pictures—photographs—fascinate me for some reason. It seemed to be an indiscriminate mess of old and new ones, and I must have spent at least an hour just trying to imagine who the people in them were. I saw the old fart in several of them, and a younger man, whom I took to be his son. There were also older ones, faded sepia, of people in Civil War garb, and late-eighteenth-century clothing. There were two photos I found particularly odd: both of Lysette, it seemed, but old, old ones, of the brown variety, of her in period costume. If it was indeed her, she must have had them done at one of those places that do old-fashioned photos—presumably as a lark or to match the other ones in the desk. I hadn't known she knew the old man. Made sense if she was a regular at the store.

There was a lot of other stuff, too. The most interesting thing I found was an acoustic guitar from the 30's, maybe earlier. It wasn't one of those shit-jobs like you see in every grampa's house, the ones that cost maybe forty bucks new and can't hold a tune. This one was hand-made with lots of inlay and no manufacturer's label. A fine piece of work, like I'd always imagined Robert Johnson might have played. I'd had some lessons in the past, and I tried to tune it up to play, but three of the strings were missing, and I couldn't get enough out of the remaining three to satisfy. I put it down and moved on. There were some interesting old books—no fiction, though—and a couple of antique rifles that might still be nice if someone took the time to sit down and clean them. Maybe later.

I looked at my watch. Two-thirty in the afternoon. Time enough for a ride up to Salt Lake City to bum around some and grab a new book before my shift.

♦ Once I got onto the freeway, a lot of old memories came flooding back. Book or not, I decided not to go anywhere specific, but just ride. It'd been a long time since I'd done that. It seemed like a long time since I'd been on the freeway for longer than just a few minutes. Actually, like I said, it had only been a year since I'd been out of action. Before that, I'd ridden with the Eliminators, an unrecognized gang that rode the Rocky Mountain area. Our primary occupations had been stealing enough to stay alive, and staying out of the Angels' way—the Angels had become all but corporate, but still didn't like any unregistered patches riding the States. We'd been doing a fair job at both until a small group of enforcers found us camped outside a little town in Nevada. I'd been one of three survivors of that raid. My gun had saved my life that day.

♦ I ran towards the house, falling heavily, knocking the breath from my lungs. But I picked myself up and kept going. I hesitated on the doorstep, the sun casting my shadow on the door, my hand frozen in mid-grasp reaching for the doorknob. At last, I opened the door and went straight for the den.

The guitar was gone.

I bet myself that when I found it, the thing wouldn't have three strings on it, but two. Damn me for not figuring it out sooner!

The house was dark and cemetery quiet. The living room yawned like the maw of a predator's cavern, and I nearly froze right then.

Could I do this?

I shook myself, and lifted the Ruger, holding in stiff in front of me like they do in cop shows, but for some reason, it didn't make me feel safer. In the dark, I wove my way through the piles of stuff I'd rearranged, feeling like a soldier in a minefield, until I neared the little hallway with that locked bedroom door. I hesitated just a moment...

I'd appreciate it if you stayed out of there.

Bluebeard's dead wives.

...before I gave it a sharp kick with the sole of my foot. The lock held fast, but the doorframe splintered with a loud crack! And I was inside.

The room was dark. Black. Of course, the damn flashlight was in the den where I'd left it.

"I've been expecting you."

I jumped. Violently. I'd been expecting the old fart to be in here, and was startled by the husky contralto of a woman.

A woman I knew.

Shit.

I had to say something. "You have?" Lame, but at least it got a response.

"Indeed I have. Though not until tonight or tomorrow. My grandson and I planned this carefully, and you've surprised me. I'll have to tell him about your quick mind." Lysette sounded pleased.

"Your grandson?" I said, doubt hanging heavy in my voice.

"The old man who hired you. He lives here occasionally. He keeps this room for me when I visit."

My God, she was serious! Her grandson? I had to buy some time, figure a way out of here. Keep her talking. "Where is he now?"

"In his condo in Palm Springs, I expect. He goes there about this time of year."

A lengthy pause, and then she said, "I've been watching you for a long time."

"And I've been reading about you for a long time."

I think I caught her off guard with that, because she went quiet again. After a second, I said, "So now what?"

She laughed, her disembodied voice more and more unnerving. I scanned the room with the .357, but found no one to point it at.

"Honestly, Nick, I'm not sure. You weren't supposed to come until later. Things are...incomplete."

"Yeah? Well, they're complete now." Good job, Nick, guess you told her with that one.

I couldn't help it. Scared to death, I counted it as luck my teeth didn't chatter.

"Yeah," she chuckled. Her laugh relaxed me a little bit, and I had to consciously remember this girl could kill me—would kill me, given half an opportunity. "I guess they are at that. One way or another."

Then I blurted, "So you really drink the blood of your victims?" Where had that come from?

She sighed heavily. "Yeah, Nick, I do. I have to eat."

I forced myself not to gag. Then, "Most people make do with steak or fried chicken," I said.

"I haven't been able to metabolize those things for over ninety years," she said. Sadness in her voice? She seemed awfully lucid for a psycho. But ninety years? She really did think she was a vampire.

I was in over my head.

At least I could try to get her out where I could deal with her on a face-to-face basis. "Um," I began. "Why don't you come out where I can see you?"

"All right," she sighed. "I guess we'll have to get this over with, won't we?"

She stepped out of the shadows, seeming to materialize from nowhere.

She was beautiful.

I've seen a lot of horror movies and a lot of Hollywood vampires, but I had no idea what to expect. Maybe a cross between Elvira, Queen of the Dark, and Morticia Addams, wearing a black dress cut to the navel and slit to the hip.

She wasn't. Lysette was still the same innocent-looking girl I'd made love to the other night. Her smile still made me feel like the only man on Earth. She wore a faded blue shirt-dress and a Marilyn Monroe "lost lamb" expression. At that moment, she was the most attractive woman I'd ever seen.

She was also a serial killer.

I swallowed, took two steps back, and leveled the Ruger at her face.

She smiled, a little sadly, I thought.

"You can't kill me, Nick."

Bonkers. "Maybe not, lady, but I'm betting if I shot you point-blank in the face, it'd slow you down long enough for me to get the hell out of here."

"Yes," she said. "It would do that. But why would you want to? I'm not going to hurt you."

"Crap."

She held up both small hands, palms out. They were empty. Then she gestured at the bed. My eyes adjusted to the dark of the room now, and I could see the old guitar lying there.

"It still has two strings on it, Nick," she said. "I'm not going to use either of them on you. I would have taken one off it by now if I were planning that."

My arms were getting tired; I wasn't used to this. The gun no longer pointed at her head, but at her belly.

"I don't buy it," I said. "You're a killer. How can I believe you won't kill me, especially since I know about your 'secret?'" I was trying to humor her, but it came out sounding sarcastic and insulting. I didn't know how to do this; I wasn't a counselor.

"You don't believe me," she said. A rock could've figured that out. "I'll show you. I want you to believe me."

"Why?"

Another long pause.

"I think I love you." It came out reluctantly, as if she couldn't believe it herself.

"Right!" I barked. I felt my lips twist into a sneer. "You damn near had me believing you."

She looked down. When she looked back at me, her eyes shone with tears.

She was good. I'll give her that.

Without a word, she went over to the window and opened the thick drapes. The skin along my spine crawled, and I tightened my grip on the Ruger. Behind the drapes, she opened louvers on a set of inner shutters. Sunlight streamed in, showing dust motes floating lazily in the air. She drew back, then gingerly pulled up one of her long sleeves to reveal a well-shaped arm. She shut her eyes, grit her teeth, and thrust the bare arm into that light.

For a few seconds, nothing happened. Then the skin where the sunlight fell reddened, then began to smoke and turn black, the way third-degree burns do. The Ruger clattered to the floor, and I rushed to pull her away from the burning sunlight. I lost my balance, and we both went onto the bed, breathing heavily like athletic lovers.

I looked down at her, stunned to see her looking like nothing more than a girl, wounded inside and out. She sobbed as she cradled her blackened arm in the other.

How could sunlight do that? There was one answer, but my mind refused to open to it. I turned and put my own hand into the beam of light. Just sunshine, pleasantly warm and somehow reassuring.

"What happened to you?" I said, maybe a bit louder than I'd intended. "Why does sunlight do that to you?"

She smiled through her tears at my density.

"Come on, Nick. You've been to the movies. You read Stoker. What did you think, I'd been lying to you? I wasn't. I've been this way for ninety years."

It was convincing, I'll say that.

"You killed all those people? Drank their blood?"

She nodded.

I looked at the floor. The Ruger rested about two yards away where I'd dropped it.

"I wasn't lying, Nick. I like you. I think I could love you. I haven't been in love for a very long time..."

"You kill people."

She could have said, so do you at that point, but to her credit, she didn't. If she had, I couldn't have denied it. She pushed herself up on her elbows on the bed. Did the blackened area seem smaller now?

"That Hispanic kid knifed three people since he arrived here. Another kid was a killer, the one responsible for a string of robbery-murders from Salt Lake to Logan. The others weren't any more innocent. You know about most of them, if you've read the papers."

"How do you know so much?" I asked.

"One of my talents, Nick. I can see into people's minds."

Ask a stupid question...

"So you set yourself up as judge and jury?"

"Can you think of anyone more qualified?" Her eyes stared through to my soul.

"What about me?" I asked. "I've killed, too. When do I die?"

"You don't. You think you're a killing machine, but you're wrong. We have a lot in common, Nick. Nicky," she said with a small sigh. "We kill when we're threatened, when we must, but never in cold blood; like predators, but tempered with judgment and conscience. I can live with that."

Nuts. She was downright nuts.

Silence fell between us for a few moments, and at some point, I found I could live with it, too. Right there, I decided I was in love with her.

She was first to break it. "We were going to run away together, Nicky. What's changed?"

Silence, again, and I thought about that. I thought about it for a long time.

Then: "Nothing," I whispered.

It was possible she wanted to kill me. It was possible she wanted to use me for her own incomprehensible goals. It was even possible she did love me.

As I said before, what the hell?

I reached for her, and she came into my arms.

We rode out after sundown.

♦

Mark W. Worthen first saw light in West Covina, California, and has since live all over the United States and all over the world. His work has appeared in various anthologies, including *Washed by a Wave of Wind* from Signature Books, *Thicker Than Water* from Tigress Press, and *Thinner Than Mist* from Bones and Caskets Press.

He currently lives with his wife, Jeannie, who is an agent and editor. Also in the house are his last remaining son (all the other children have moved out) and a dog. He (Mark, not the dog) is currently at work on his second novel, a full-length story featuring Nick and Lysette.

www.markwworthen.com

Mark W. Worthen

"Julie Broise and the Devil"

by Seanan McGuire

Julie always needed more than anyone could give her. Offer her a dime and she'd want a dollar; offer her a rhyme and she'd demand the whole song. That's how she was made. She wasn't good at knowing her limits, and unless you know your own limits, you'll never know anybody else's. But I guess Julie taught us that better than anybody dreamed she could.

We were in the middle of an interesting patch here in Rush's Bend when the business with Julie came around. Between the Hilliard girl turning out a werewolf and Michael Jones refusing to let us cut down any of the trees until he figured out which one used to be his girlfriend, most of us hadn't had a wink of sleep in months. Seemed every kid in town had to wake their parents to ask "Papa, did you find me in a tree stump?" or "Mama, was there a summer storm when I got born?" Even my Applejack woke me with questions, and you'd think she'd know her purpose by now, being a Tucker and all.

It was a right mess. Every generation has a few oddities, like my older brother who went off to help the phantom lumbermen clear a path from the underworld to the Rio Grande, or Uncle Abram, who married a mermaid. But when folks start inviting the strangeness in, it gets a bit more...common. Sometimes it even gets a little pushy about getting what it wants. And in those days, there wasn't a single girl in town pushier about getting what she wanted than Julie Broise.

The Broises have lived in Rush's Bend almost as long as anybody. Julie's mama was a Lewis, and city-born, even though she's never talked about it much. She came to Rush's Bend alone when she was just a little girl, moving in with her grandparents on the edge of the swamp forest. No one knows why she came to live with her folks here, although there've been guesses. Abigail herself has never said a word.

Most of us knew Abigail would marry Autonomy Broise from the day she got here, even though they were both of them scarce nine years old; they had that kind of love between them. Any worries about Autonomy falling for a city girl faded the first time folks saw Abigail dancing barefoot by the swamp's edge, swaying in time to the frog songs, with will o' wisps tangled in her hair. Abigail's always belonged in Rush's Bend, even if she wasn't born here. When she came to live with her father's parents, she was coming home.

But Julie…if anyone was meant to live far from here, it was her. She had too much fire and spite in her to be happy in a little town where everyone knows everyone else, including all the family ghosts. She needed bright lights and loud noises and glitter and change, and maybe if she'd gotten them, things would've been different.

Not that you'd know how she was just looking at her! She was even prettier than her mama, with big doe's eyes and long brown hair she kept braided with daisies. There's never been a girl used so many daisies in her hair; she could've picked the fields clean all by herself. Buttercup Hilliard used to yell something awful about all the daisies Julie picked. "How're the rest of us supposed to fetch the boys if she takes all the flowers before we can make ourselves as pretty as she is?" she'd ask, and no one could answer her—but no one could make Julie stop picking daisies, either.

It didn't help that Julie was built just as delicate as those daisies, with a soft, small waist, and soft, small hands that never did a lick of work. Her real problem was that she knew how pretty she was, and pretty only lasts as long as it doesn't know what it is. You tell pretty what kind of power it's got, and the first thing it does is start finding ways to turn itself sour. That's why enchanted princesses are pretty, but you never hear about pretty evil queens. They can be beautiful—beauty has different rules—but they burn the pretty out of themselves with their plotting and conniving.

Julie might have been the prettiest girl in Rush's Bend, but she was also the meanest. She caught all the boys, but she lost them as quick as she caught them, once they learned that she could tan a hide with nothing but the edges on her tongue. The other girls might've saved her from herself if they'd been willing, but none of them was after she'd taken off with all their boyfriends, not even Contingency Jones. That's where the trouble started. Here was Julie Broise, pretty as a picture and mean as a swamp rat, going around breaking the boys' hearts and making the girls hate her. Eventually there wasn't anyone left in the whole town that didn't think she was a nasty, spiteful little thing. Even her own momma and poppa shook their heads when they thought she wasn't looking, wondering if they hadn't somehow fetched up with a changeling child. Abigail still danced by the swamp at moonrise and Autonomy still watched her, but they never stopped wondering what got left out of their little girl when they made her. They never did figure it out. A lot of folks believe that's why Julie was their only child.

It was a fine spring day when Julie decided to go walking along the stream, after she'd worn out her welcome at home by refusing to help her momma with the chores. She put on her nicest skirts and wrapped her shawl around her shoulders and went to see if there was anyone that would go walking out with her. She knew what folks said when they thought she couldn't hear, but she was still the prettiest girl around—and men, she knew, would forgive an awful lot for a pretty girl.

The first person she found was Paul McKinsey. He was a big boy then, and he's bigger now, but he turned bright red when he saw her looking. Paul and Julie had never gone walking out; he had the freckles for five boys and ears you could use for handles, and he knew that if she was looking at him, it was because she'd hit the bottom of the barrel...but that didn't stop his ears from burning when she smiled.

Julie knew what it meant when a boy turned that color, and Paul wasn't so bad; he had a nice smile and thick hair, and freckles didn't matter in the dark. Maybe he wasn't as good a catch as Willie Taylor, but he'd do. She started sauntering up to him, smooth and sleek as a hunting cat, but stopped when Buttercup Hilliard walked up and took his arm, proprietary as you please.

Buttercup gave her a smile that would've been sweet as fresh cream if it hadn't had so many teeth in it. Folks and wolves have different smiles, and when the folks are wolves, well..."Julie. I didn't know you'd be out today. You stepping out with someone, or just wandering on your lonesome?"

Julie smiled back. "I'm stepping out. I just ain't sure who I'm stepping with. Someone's bound to come along." She flashed Paul a smoldering smile that said volumes about who she thought "someone" would be.

Paul swallowed a yelp as Buttercup's hand tightened on his arm. He was a bright boy and he knew she didn't mean to hurt him; a few bruises are part and parcel of stepping out with a werewolf. That and knowing better than to even think about hitting your dogs.

"Good luck finding someone," Buttercup said, words holding just the hint of a growl. "Pretty thing like you shouldn't have any trouble."

"I doubt I will," said Julie, eyes still on Paul. "Just about everybody in town's been glad to walk out with me one time or another."

Paul didn't like this line of talking. He glanced at Buttercup, and saw she had her eyes fixed on Julie's throat like it was a fresh-baked batch of her momma's bread. That settled things. He didn't want to be caught between them, but even more, he didn't want to explain to Julie's parents why he'd just stood there while his girl took their daughter down like a deer. "Buttercup, we should get going, unless we want to get to the woods and find them hunted out," he said, as fast as he could.

"Going hunting?" Julie asked, sweet as pie. "That's nice. I like to see things boys and girls can do together. 'Course, I don't hunt none."

Buttercup growled, her grip on Paul's arm tightening. He was ready to bolt, whether or not Buttercup went with him; he could see where Julie was heading, and he really didn't want to go on that trip. "Julie," he said, warningly, "I wouldn't—"

"But that's because I never hit anything I shoot at." Julie tossed him a flirtatious glance. "What'd you think I was going to say, something about not liking the fur in my teeth? Shame on you! You should think better of your girl." She turned and sashayed away, putting an extra little toss into her hips as she heard Buttercup's growl deepen. Paul would spend the rest of the afternoon digging his way out of that little mess, and that suited Julie just fine—just fine indeed.

Of course, revenge didn't make her any less alone. Julie started to do a slow burn of her own as she walked. How dare he brush her off! What did a smelly old werewolf have that she didn't, besides the fleas and ticks? There was a time when Paul would've died for the chance to walk out with her, but there he'd been, dismissing her without a hint of regret. Well, she'd show him; she'd never offer to walk out with him again, and he could stay the only boy in town she'd never shown any favor to. That'd teach him.

What Julie didn't know was that things had changed. There was a time when Paul would've gladly walked out with her, because she was pretty and soft to look at even if she was sharp and cruel to talk to, and walking out with her would show the other girls he was worth a second look. But once he'd found Buttercup, well...Julie was still pretty and soft to look at, but he didn't need that anymore. He needed a girl who understood him and who he understood—and if Buttercup was a wolf sometimes, he understood that well enough. Julie understood pretty words and pretty things, and courting someone just to have them on your arm; what she didn't understand was giving wilted daisies and clumsy poetry, or why her father went to the swamp to watch her mother dance. For Julie, there was always another boy when the one you had was used up and went away.

As Julie walked along the path, head held high to hide the anger in her heart, she heard splashing and laughter coming from the river. Whoever it was sounded like they were having a grand old time, and Julie got it in her head to go and join the fun. After all, she thought, there was enough water for everyone. So she slipped into the bushes and sidled along until she reached the riverbank and found herself looking at Contingency Jones and Washington Dunn, both of them naked as jaybirds as they played in the stream.

Now neither, of them had seen her; they just kept splashing around calling each other silly names, the way young lovers do. Maybe you or I would've smiled and crept away, seeing it was a private sort of game and not wanting to spoil their fun, but not Julie. She put two fingers in her mouth and whistled, bringing their laughter to a sudden stop. Contingency sunk down in the water until all you could see was her head and the frown she was suddenly wearing.

"Why, Julie Broise," she said, sounding almost ill. "We didn't see you there."

"I didn't think you did," said Julie, flirting her eyelashes at Washington just like he wasn't standing in his altogether in hip-deep water.

Washington may never win any prizes for brains—comes of being part bear on his daddy's side—but he's bright enough to know right from wrong. He knew it was Contingency who'd come to his door with a basket of gooseberry tarts and a shy smile, and it was Contingency he'd spent the summer courting. And maybe it was the bear in him, but he'd take Contingency's dull-honey hair over Julie's chestnut brown any day. He folded his arms, glaring at Julie, and said, "It's not nice to sneak up on people."

"Heavens, Washington, I didn't sneak! I was just coming down to sit and think a bit; it's not my fault you and your little friend—hello, Contingency—decided to have a bath." She flashed Contingency a smile as false as the gilt paint on a carnival wonder-wagon. She could see how red the other girl's ears were turning, burning with guilt and embarrassment over being caught in such a childish game.

But Washington never learned that grown-ups should be embarrassed about playing children's games, and he liked to watch Contingency in the water. When she swam she looked like she was flying, and since his favorite things were birds and her, seeing Contingency fly was about the nicest thing in the world. With Julie there, Contingency wasn't flying. He wanted her to start again. "Maybe you should go find someplace else to think. There's a lot of stream. I bet there's somewhere nicer."

"Don't you like my company?" Julie asked. "Come on, Washington. I'm awful lonely, and you look like you're having a good time. Could I join you?"

If it was all right for Contingency to go swimming with him, Washington supposed it had to be all right for Julie. He turned, meaning to ask if she minded Julie joining them—and found Contingency was gone. He peered into the water, giving a poor frog the scare of its life…but still, there was no Contingency.

He looked up. "Where'd she go?"

Julie smirked. She'd seen Contingency sink down, and she knew the girl had swum downstream to find a place where she could leave the water without being seen. Contingency might be the nicest girl in town, but she was also one of the shyest, and if she was willing to let Washington see her swimming around without a stitch on, it was because they'd been walking out together for months. There was no way she'd let Julie, with her perfect prettiness and her sharp tongue, go on seeing her that way.

"Looks like she's left," Julie said, voice dripping with sympathy. "I guess she didn't want to play. But I'll play with you." She slid out of her shawl, dipping one toe into the stream. "I'll be glad to."

"I don't want to play with you," he said, looking back into the water. "I want to play with Contingency. Contingency! Where are you?"

Now Contingency hadn't gone far—she was shy but she wasn't stupid, and there was no way she'd go and leave her fella alone with Julie Broise. She'd hid behind a patch of cattails, watching furiously as she waited for Julie to make her move. But when she heard him calling her and ignoring Julie, well...she barely kept from whooping aloud with the sheer joy of it. She dove down under the water and came up again right in front of Washington, laughing.

"Here I am, honey," she said, and spread her arms. "Catch me if you can!" And she dove and swam as fast as she could, and Washington followed, leaving Julie standing on the bank and trying to figure out what had just happened. She knew she was the prettier of the two: she had big dark eyes and long soft hair, and she knew how to smile and move and make a fella feel like he was her whole world. What she couldn't understand was that when Contingency burst out of the water with her heavy thighs and chapped hands, she was the most beautiful thing Washington Dunn had ever seen, and that because he thought she was beautiful, she was, if only for him.

Julie picked up her shawl, fuming and fuming as she tied it around her shoulders. How dare he choose Contingency over her? She had the better family and stood to have a richer dowry; Contingency just had thick ankles and a reputation for the best bread in town. It wasn't fair.

Nose in the air, she stalked away from the stream, putting them behind her.

She wound through the trees instead of climbing back up the path; no Rush's Bend girl has ever been put off by something as trivial as the possibility of mud or frogs, and Julie was no different. She was born and bred here, just like the rest of us. Maybe if she'd understood that, she'd have come off a little better.

She'd been walking through the trees near half a mile when she heard someone playing the banjo inside the old willow grove. We've had some fine banjo players up here—not as many as we've had guitarists, more than we've had harpists—and all of them have had a style of their own, but the playing Julie heard wasn't familiar in the slightest. Every note rang pure and true, and she knew that if there'd been anyone with that style of play anywhere in town, she'd have heard them before. But she hadn't, and that told her she'd found my Applejack.

The dead know all the best songs, but they can only play them through living hands, and that meant they needed Applejack Tucker. Most people would stop and listen for a spell if they found Applejack playing a ghost-tune, warm their hearts up on the music and move along, never letting her know they'd been there. Not Julie. She walked around that briar three times before she found a pathway through the thorns, picked the brambles apart with a stick, and walked on in, just as bold as brass.

There sat Applejack with her eyes closed, fingers gliding over the strings of her old banjo. Whoever was riding that time was kind, because her fingers slowed and stilled while Julie watched, cradling that instrument like a mother cradles her child.

"That's enough, little girl," Applejack said, voice pitched low in the back of her throat. "You'll run yourself raw if you don't stop." She paused and answered back in her own higher, sweeter tone, saying, "It's all right, sir, really, I won't hurt m'self. I can play hours yet."

"Maybe you can," Julie said, "but would anyone want to hear it if you did?"

Applejack's head snapped up, eyes still shut, and her hands tightened on the banjo. "Who're you, girl?" she demanded, tone dropping back to that low, deep register. Anyone with half a brain would've known that little picker-girl was being ghost-ridden, and Julie wasn't stupid; she just didn't care. She knew a ghost couldn't hurt anyone it wasn't riding, and more, she knew that if whoever was riding Applejack let go of the banjo, he'd let go of the girl as well. He could hurt Applejack before he went, but that didn't bother Julie none. She'd had a rotten day, and she was feeling mean.

"Julie Broise, as you well know, Applejack," she said, stressing the girl's proper name. "Are you playing ghost-games again? Everyone knows there's no such things."

The man in Applejack's skin gave a low moan, and Applejack broke in, her voice ringing clear and furious: "Don't you go saying things like that, Julie Broise! You know as well as I do that there are so ghosts, and there's no call for you to be rude to 'em just because they're dead!"

"I'll say what I want to who I want, and that includes you, Applejack Tucker. How many times you need me to say it?" Ghosts don't like to hear that they don't exist. It hurts. And when that ghost has already been burning all its energy to borrow a body, well, it doesn't take too many "no such things" to knock that ghost clean loose. "There just ain't no such thing!"

Applejack's fingers raked the banjo strings in a discordant jangle, and her eyes snapped open, glaring cold and furious. "What'd you go and do that for?" she demanded. "Huh? Why'd you need to go and do that? It took me weeks to get him to come out and play! They burned him for a witch for his playin'! Time was he wouldn't need me, but he needs me now—how's he supposed to play if you make him afraid to come out?"

If Julie felt bad for what she'd done, she didn't show it. She laughed as she said, "Shoot, Applejack, everyone knows that banjo of yours ain't nothing magic; it's just some old thing you dug out of a well-earned retirement. You're just looking for a little extra attention with all these ghost stories of yours."

The look Applejack gave her was half bitter and half sad, and Julie flinched; she could stand almost anything but pity. "You really don't know, do you? I'm sorry for that, but I won't stand for you callin' my guests names. Don't go doing that, hear me? Do it again, well...I won't be so inclined to forgive you." And she tossed her hair like she was the Queen of Fairy herself and went stalking off, cradling her banjo in her arms.

By that point Julie was starting to get a mite confused. What was going on, if even the ghosts and the werewolves had people to walk with, while she was all alone? Nothing good, that was sure. And there was Applejack. Julie knew as well as anyone that Applejack was a Tucker—an honest-to-goodness medium—even if all her ghost talking was through her banjo. She knew what Applejack did was real, and necessary. So why was she so full of the need to taunt her?

She walked over and sat down on Applejack's stump, resting her chin on her knuckles. Shoot, it seemed like the whole town had gone nuts. So what if she was a little sharp sometimes? Wasn't she prettier and smarter than they were? Didn't she know the way things were supposed to be better than anybody else? So what if she couldn't dance the will o' wisps out of the swamp the way her momma could, or get the rocks and trees to sing with her like Applejack did? She was as good as anybody else in Rush's Bend.

"Better, even," she said, sounding sour and cross even to herself. The fact of the matter was that she was lonely, and getting lonelier. The boys she'd stepped out with the summer before were settling down with girls of their own—sensible, friendly girls who might not be as pretty as Julie, but who wouldn't toss them aside like wilted daisies the first time they said or thought something that wasn't the way Julie wanted it. And while their little brothers didn't have girls of their own yet, she was lonely, not desperate. They were still children, and she was a woman in the brightness of her bloom.

Besides, she thought, she could have any man in Rush's Bend, married or not, if she was willing to deal with the consequences of chasing after the ones that already had wives. Some of the wives wouldn't be any trouble. Others, though…she suppressed a shudder as she thought of what would happen if she made a serious play for any man foolish enough to marry Buttercup Hilliard. Part of being able to have was having the common sense to know which ones weren't worth having. She could let one go off to deal with fleas and ticks and a wife who'd have puppies instead of babies. Given time enough, when she'd found a man that she could stand, she'd make a bride out of herself.

I'm sure there are lots of places where a story like this would end right here, and that's fine. I'd bet most of those places, while they may have their own kind of local color, don't have quite the same clashing local rainbow as Rush's Bend. The town sits on an edge in the world, and it seems just about every strange thing you ever went looking for winds up here, sooner or later. As Julie sat there, thinking bitter thoughts about every other girl and boy in town, she came to one of those edges. And she stepped off.

I'm sure any one of you—bright folks that you are— would have realized what it meant when you smelled brimstone on that lovely summer breeze. And then, depending on what you believed was the right way to do things, you might've made the sign of the cross or played a silver flute or tossed a handful of salt over your shoulder, and that would've been that. Most devils can't stand being warded off, any more than ghosts can stand being told they don't exist.

But Julie was a forward-thinking young woman, even though she lived in a place as backwards-existing as Rush's Bend, and when she smelled that sulfur, she just ignored it and kept thinking bitter thoughts, as self-absorbed and careless as ever.

"Julie Broise?" said a voice behind her, smooth as satin and twice as slippery.

"You know I am," she said automatically, before she realized she'd never heard that voice before. Rush's Bend isn't very big. By the time you're about six years old, you know every voice there is to know, and strangers are a rare enough occurrence that they rarely manage to go anywhere alone. But this was no voice Julie had ever heard before; this was someone altogether new. She felt a little thrill run down her back, and shivered, not entirely from excitement, as she turned to study the stranger.

He was dressed like some sort of traveling salesman, but all in black, save for the brightly colored brim of his jaunty straw hat. It wasn't sitting quite even: one of his horns was pushing it off-center. Most places, folks look at a man with horns and run. But Julie was raised in Rush's Bend, and while she may not have learned to be polite, she surely learned to be tolerant. Pretty hard not to be, considering the folks that live here.

"How'd you get here?" she demanded, because while she might be polite enough not to run, that didn't make her civil. "I've been sitting right here, and that," she pointed, "is the only way in, and I sure didn't see you walk up!"

Now the Devil—because that's who it was, just as sure as springtime—was getting his first view of Julie Broise, and it was Julie at her best. Maybe a normal man would look at her, arrogant and angry, and think about finding a sweeter example of the fair sex. But for him, well, seeing her with her shoulders squared and her nostrils flaring…he couldn't have conceived a fairer woman if he'd tried. And he _had_ tried, but the fact of it was, he'd heard about the edge on her tongue and the way she could bite the hand that fed her, and he'd gotten it into his head to come a-courting.

"Well, ma'am," he said, "you were only watching straight ahead. There are other directions a body can come from."

"Really?" she said. "Around here, people mostly keep to straight lines." And if that wasn't an untruth, considering the ruckus the summer before about Contingency's brother Cunning and his homemade wings, well, there isn't much that's false.

"I suppose so," said the Devil. "But still, Miss Broise, I'm pleased as can be to make your acquaintance, straight lines or not. I've come a fair way to meet you."

Julie paused. Most strangers that came to town—and this one was as strange as they came—had never heard of her. She smiled at him, feeling a good bit more kindly than she had a moment before. "Why, thank you," she said. Nobody could fault her manners, when she was of a mind to use them. "And you would be...?"

"That doesn't matter, just now. Would you like to walk out with me for a bit, Miss Julie Broise?"

If that didn't just about beat all! Not only did this stranger come knowing who she was, he had the good sense to want to walk with her. She rose, offering her arm, and said, "That would surely be a lovely way to pass an afternoon."

I wish I could say no one in town knew what was happening, and no doubt everyone who was there that day wishes the same. But Buttercup and her brothers smelled the brimstone, and Washington felt his grandfather's blood rising in him like ice, and Applejack's banjo played a few lost, lonely notes, even though no hands were near the strings.

That might have been enough, on another day, and maybe Applejack would have sounded the alarm. She could've come chasing down with all her chants and charms, and driven that demon clean away from Julie. But Julie made Applejack's ghost-rider mighty angry;

he'd have a while to wait before he could ride that little picker-girl and play her banjo again, and it burned him up inside. So when the banjo started to sing warning, he used what little power he had and pressed those strings silent as the grave. Applejack looked up, and frowned, and looked away, and the moment to save Julie was lost forever.

Some folks say I see everything that happens here, and for the most part, they're right, but there are things I don't see, and among them is the conversation between Julie Broise and the Devil. She'd called him by hating and wanting and being so spiteful no one else would want to court her—but young girls are always bringing up devils, whether they know it or not. All I know is that when Julie Broise called up her own particular devil she took his arm and they walked together onto whatever path is given for spiteful girls and the demons who come courting them. And that was all.

That night, when Abigail Broise put down her broom and walked to the edge of the swamp, she found her daughter's shawl discarded on the ground. She looked at it a long while before she turned and walked back to town. She came back with her husband, and the neighbors from every side, until the whole town was gathered, just looking at that poor scrap of wool. It was clean enough, save for the streak of ashes down one side, like it had got too close to the fire. No one said where those ashes came from—not out loud—but then, they didn't have to.

Folks tried to look sorry, but the truth is, most weren't. Julie was never careful or stingy about where she applied the edge of her tongue, and people could be forgiven if losing her didn't seem like the worst hardship they'd ever endured. A few folks really were sorry. The ones who smelled the brimstone or saw the signs coming, and not done a thing to stop it. And that, too, was as it ought to be.

We buried her shawl in the churchyard. Her father planted an ash tree on her grave; it's young yet, but it'll grow, and the will o' wisps gather in its branches at night. No one really thinks she's dead, but sometimes it helps if you pretend, and maybe the Devil got what he deserved when he took our Julie.

Applejack probably put it best—or maybe one of her riders did. It's hard to tell with that girl. I like to think it was the ghost who stopped her banjo from giving warning, but we may never know. She sang:

"The Devil came to Rush's Bend, out searching for a bride,
A woman that would suit him in her beauty and her pride.
The Devil searched the whole wide world
before he made a choice,
And then he came and carried off our own fair Julie Broise.

Now Julie wasn't soft, unless you like a raging stream,
And Julie wasn't kind, unless you like the touch of steam,
And Julie wasn't warm, unless you like embracing fire,
And all the things she wasn't made her his one true desire.

So no one here's seen Julie since the day the Devil came—
We figure that she's married him and taken on his name.
But here's the part we can't quite guess
and nobody can tell—
Why the hell'd he need our Julie? He already had Hell."

♦

Seanan McGuire, a native Californian, is afraid of weather and remarkably laid-back about rattlesnakes. This sideways sensibility informs everything she does, from studying folklore to collecting horror movies and reading books about infectious disease. And, of course, writing.

Seanan is the author of the *October Daye* series of urban fantasies, the first seven of which have been purchased by DAW Books; the *InCryptid* series of urban fantasies, the first two of which have been purchased by DAW Books; and the *Newsflesh* trilogy, published by Orbit under the pseudonym "Mira Grant." She's working on several other books, just to make sure she never runs out of things to edit. Her short fiction has appeared in multiple anthologies, and she was a 2010 Universe Author for *The Edge of Propinquity*.

In her spare time, Seanan writes and records original music. Most people believe that she doesn't sleep.

www.seananmcguire.com

"Sane Reaction"

By Lisa Morton

Anne leads him through the front door of the duplex, keys still jingling in one hand. She glances around nervously, wrinkles her nose slightly.

"It's a little…messy," she stammers, "and I forgot to take the garbage out this morning, so please excuse the…you know. "

John sniffs the air, but detects only pine and lemon, air freshener and cleanser. He sees her flutter at an already-tidy stack of mail on a table by the door, and has to laugh. "It's okay, really. I can handle it."

She tries to return his smile, then watches uncertainly as he strides past her into the living room. She locks the front door, then follows.

He's in the middle of the room, examining the Brian Davis floral prints hung beneath the 1930's ceiling molding, the crowded entertainment center, the pastel couch and chairs, coffee table, scattered papers and magazines.

He completes his circuit of the room and turns to her approvingly. "This is nice, I mean it. In fact, what do you pay here? If you don't mind my asking?"

"Nine-fifty, plus utilities."

"No roommate?," he asks carefully.

"No roommate," she grimaces slightly, "I've done my roommate time already. Of course I've been here for five years now, and we have rent control."

He glances around once more, then turns that critical eye on her. "Just like I pictured it."

Anne realizes she's still clutching her purse, and she sets it down in its usual spot on the chair by the wall. She feels slightly uncomfortable—she'd say 'naked', but it sounds so clichéd—under the weight of John's assessment, but she tries to sound nonchalant when she answers, "Really? I wouldn't have thought you'd had time to 'picture it'."

John takes a step closer to her, his eyes never leaving her face. "Oh, it's a little game I play, you know, in my head. Whenever I meet someone new, I always try to figure them out first—what their place'll look like, what kind of music they're into, that kind of thing. I'm usually right, too."

He turns to indicate the framed posters, then picks up a CD cover, reading over the artist's name and album title. "With you I guessed the floral prints, new age instrumentals and lots of refrigerator magnets."

"Yeah, well," she returns, as she steps up and plucks the CD from his fingers, "you were wrong there. I only have one refrigerator magnet."

She steps around him to slide the disc into the player, John admiring the movements of her long, slender fingers. The resulting music is synthesized, sampled, sensual. They both sway to it slightly, until he steps forward, as if intending to pull her into a real dance.

She backs away involuntarily, then smiles to hide her embarrassment. "Ah, how about a drink?"

"Sure," John responds sarcastically, "that's what we're here for, right?"

When she doesn't come back, he adds, "What've you got?"

"Vodka."

"Stoli, I hope. No Absolut."

Anne tries to decide if he's serious or not, then gives up on figuring him out and says simply, "Sorry. It's a generic brand."

"Generic, huh?," John responds with a moue of disappointment.

Then he saunters towards her, and she wills herself to stay, remembering what they are here for. "Um-hmm."

He puts his arms around her, without force, a soft motion. "Well, there's a bad habit I'll have to change."

"Oh you will, will you?"

He's bending down, tilting his head, but when she sees the slight smile still on his lips, she abruptly pulls away and slides gracefully to the doorway. She pauses there, just long enough to offer her own coy grin. "I'll get our drinks."

John lets her go, appreciating her new understanding of the game. He absentmindedly picks up a newspaper, sees it's a week old and features a headline about the death toll in the latest natural disaster. He calls out in the direction of the kitchen, "So how'd you find out about Eileen's parties? Do you know her?"

Anne doesn't look up from the ice cube trays as she cracks them. "Eileen who?"

"Guess that answers that question," John notes to himself, setting the paper down, then raising his voice to her, "We met at her introduction party tonight, remember?"

"Oh, *that* Eileen."

Anne reappears with two small glasses, one of which she passes to him. He accepts it with raised eyebrows. "Ikea glasses. I guessed that, too."

She watches as he downs half the contents of the glass in one gulp, then she raises her own for a small sensible sip.

John flops heavily onto the couch, spreading his arms along the back as if measuring the extent of his property, holding the glass balanced there.

"So, about Eileen..."

"Oh, right." Anne moves to the far end of the couch and perches on the arm. "No, I went with a friend who found out about these singles parties from the classifieds in the back of City magazine."

"And, you abandoned your friend to leave with a stranger?"

"My friend abandoned me first."

"Oh." He tastes the vodka again and looks away.

"What about you? Did you read the same ad?"

"No," John responds, "in my case Eileen is a friend. She doesn't even charge me."

"So, I guess I'm a freebie, huh?"

John does look at her now, sharply, then he sets his empty glass on the coffee table, rises and walks the length of the couch to her. "No, no. I'd like to think there are some things money can't buy."

Anne eyes his leather jacket, smells his expensive cologne, and again wonders if he's truthful or toying. "What else do you like?"

He leans over her, supporting himself with one arm against the sofa back. He's so close she feels his warm breath on her hair when he murmurs, "Women who make a habit of picking up men they don't know at parties."

Anne barks out a disbelieving laugh and slides out from under him. "Oh, wait a minute, who said I 'make a habit' of this?"

"Don't you?"

She turns away, feeling the heat rise to her cheeks. "As a matter of fact I've…well, I've…never done this before."

"You haven't?"

"No," she begins, pacing around the couch, "usually I have to know someone for a long time before I do…this. Like my last boyfriend, Kenny. We saw each other nearly every day for a year at work before we ever went out."

"And what happened to Kenny?"

"What do you mean?," she blurts out, turning to watch his response with something like suspicion.

"I mean, why'd you break up?"

She sighs, lowers herself onto the chair next to her purse. "Oh, we'd been together long enough to know it wasn't working out."

"And how long was that?"

"Two weeks."

She joins John's laughter, then is finishing her own drink, when he notes, "You sound like you make up your mind fast."

"No sense in beating a dead horse, right?"

Her tone is unmistakably flirtatious, and John rises, goes to her, finds she doesn't resist as he pries the glass from her hand, sets it down. "Especially when there are more interesting things…"

She lets him put his arms around her and asks, "What about you? Is this your preferred method of meeting girls?"

John considers. "Well, to tell you the truth, yes, it is."

She pulls back, actually surprised. "Really?"

John watches as some shadow crosses her features, and he reluctantly relinquishes his hold.

"At least you're honest. Kenny wasn't. Neither was Aaron."

John, sensing this is her last line of defense, plays along. "Aaron?"

"The one before Kenny. I caught him with one of my best friends."

"Very nice," John interjects with what he hopes is the right amount of disgust.

A small silence follows, and John intuits that the queen in this match has just been checked. He lets his eyes obviously consume her, imagining the lean muscles beneath the tight jeans and silk blouse. She smiles when she looks away this time, her gaze settling on his empty glass. "Can I get you another?"

"Generic? Thanks, no?"

"What a critic! So much for hospitality."

Maybe it's the way she puts a hand on one hip during her mock outrage, or the way her eyes seem half-lidded when she tilts her head back. In any case, John knows he's won. Checkmate.

"Why don't you show me some *real* hospitality?"

"Real, huh?" She appears to consider, then drops her shoulders as if acknowledging defeat, surrender. "Okay."

She approaches him this time, puts her arms around his neck, pulls his head down for the first kiss. It's tentative, cautious, and he pulls back easily.

"Now what would your mother say if she knew her little girl had picked up her first strange man at a party?"

"She'd probably think it was about par for her strange little girl," she slurs, pulling him down again.

But, he only brushes her lips, moving his mouth instead along her cheek, down her jaw line to neck, up to one ear. She closes her eyes and gives herself over, not even noticing when his tongue lingers too long on the lobe.

"You have pierced ears," he breathes.

She barely reacts to the comment, gasping instead as his tongue circles the inner rim of her ear.

"How old were you when you had it done?"

Her eyes flutter but don't open, even though his suddenly strange words war with the physical sensations created by his mouth.

"Uh...sixteen, I think."

His breath hot on the ring in the lobe, he asks, "Were you still a virgin?"

Now, her eyes do open, but his hands are on her head, holding it. Even the new age instrumental seems to shift to something no longer soft, lulling. "What?"

"Did it turn you on?" he asks, ignoring her alarm in his arousal. "You know, get you off?"

She jerks her head back out of his grasp, but he moves with a swiftness surprising in such a large man, encircling her narrow waist completely with one arm, still massaging her ear with the other.

"No."

His eyes are glazed, his respiration quickening. "Too bad. It would have if I had done it for you."

He seems unaware of her squirming in his grip, continuing the seduction with both tongue and touch. "First, I would have taken an ice cube and rubbed it on the lobe, until it was numb and tingling. Then, the needle, going into the soft flesh, slowly, twirling slightly. Then, when the needle was all the way through, and the hole made, I would have put my mouth up to it and sucked the blood away."

He leans down to kiss the ear again, but she dodges the move, and instead he finally looks into her face as if gauging the effect of his foreplay.

So, she tells him. "That's sick."

"How do you know? Have you tried it that way? We could do it here, tonight. A lot of people have their ears pierced twice." His fingers move from her ear to the corner of her mouth. "Or, we could do the tongue." Then, before she can stop it, the hand is on her breast, squeezing through the silk. "Or, a nipple."

He tightens his arm around her, and when she feels the erection, she puts both hands on his chest, trying to push him away. "Look, I don't think this—"

"C'mon, I thought you wanted me," John grins mirthlessly, grinding his hips against her.

She tries to move from side to side, panic spilling out in her words. "I did. I mean, you weren't like this at the party."

"You didn't get to know me very well at the party, did you?"

And with that, he throws his arms wide, releasing her, daring her.

She looks around frantically, sees the doorway leading out, away, and takes the dare. But, she's forgotten how fast he moves, and he catches her easily, hurling her into the entertainment unit in one smooth motion.

Her back impacts painfully with a hard wooden shelf, and the CD jams in the player, repeating one shrill note over and over. It sounds like gunfire.

BAM...BAM...BAMBAMBAM...

John leaps forward and grabs the player, ignoring the sparks that explode out as he hurls the unit across the room to crash against a floral print. Then, he takes Anne in the same way and throws her to the couch.

She lands and twists her head, a new agony in her neck flaring to join the one in her back. She doesn't even wipe away her tears, but watches him through them, trying to make herself small against the cushions.

"Why don't you just try to relax a little?" he tells her coolly, appraising her. "You might actually enjoy it. The others did."

He takes the leather jacket off and lays it carefully out on the coffee table. Then, as he works at his retro gold cufflinks, he circles the couch confidently, sure of his ability to prevent any escape.

"The others?" Anne can't make her head turn, but she tries to follow his movements from the corners of her eyes.

"Yeah. All the other little girls from all the other parties—and singles ads, and dating services, and dark overpriced bars. Oh, they screamed, even through their gags." He bends down from behind and clamps a hand to her mouth. Then, he moves the hand down teasingly, caressing her tight, tense shoulders.

"But it's so hard to tell a scream of pain from one of pleasure, isn't it?"

"How many others?" she asks in a small voice.

John leaves off the caresses to consider, walking around to the front of the couch, where she sees he's gotten the cufflinks off and is working on the buttons.

"I don't know. I forget."

"You don't know Eileen, do you?"

"Eileen?" He smiles in appreciation of some private joke. "Afraid we haven't had the pleasure, yet."

He turns his back to her again, searching for something in his jacket, and her eyes leave him to weigh the possibilities. The path to the exit is clear, if she can just outrun him. She thinks of the knives in the kitchen—

—and leaps to her feet. But once more he catches her effortlessly. She tries to lash out at him, and succeeds in inadvertently scratching his cheek.

John feels the sting of her nails, his eyes widen in surprise and rage, his arm comes up and swings back, and he backhands her powerfully. She flies to the floor, landing on the old Persian rug, too dazed to be grateful for that much. Black stars implode in her vision, slowly turning purple.

John looks down, sees her unfocused eyes and the trickle of blood from her cracked lip. He pulls off his shirt, tosses it onto the couch, then settles to his knees over her, straddling her.

When the stars finally fade to pain, Anne realizes she's seeing two things.

One is the tattoo on his chest. It's a figure, crucified, but wholly without religious intent, because the thing is demonic, deathly, hollow banshee face shrieking into a blistering wind, tinted rags blowing around a skeletal body. The bony hands end precisely at each of his nipples, and the thick length of metal that crucifies them is real, embedded in his own flesh. A final stud crucifies both the ghoul's feet and John's navel. The chest is clearly shaven, the prickly stubble only adding to the terror of the entire creation.

The second thing Anne has noticed is the erection, pressing even more harshly against the cloth of his pants.

"You've probably heard of me."

She can only gape, all too aware of her pain and his threat.

He glances at the paper on the nearby table. "Fucking papers. They're the ones who gave me that name: 'the Picasso Killer'. But they won't give me a headline. Shit." For a moment, he looks genuinely disappointed, then he shifts his gaze back to her, grinning. "Still, it means they know me."

As Anne's overtaxed mind makes the connection, he sees first terror, then a strange fascination wash over her.

"You're him."

Pleased at her recognition, he bends down over her. "Yeah. See, you do know me. All of you do. And none of you are gonna forget me, either."

John remembers what he was searching his jacket for, and he stands, leaving her to crawl the two feet to the couch, where she props herself up, trying to regain strength, calm.

"And it's not really such a terrible name, I guess," he muses while rifling the jacket, "because I am an artist at what I do. And, because the way I left the third one, she looked like an abstract painting. Maybe even Cubist."

He stops talking, having found what he was lacking. Anne can't see what it is yet, his broad back blocking her view, but to keep from finding out, she knows she needs to keep him talking. "They say you've killed twelve…"

He smiles in satisfaction. "But, ya know what, little girl? That's just the ones they've found. The ones I wanted them to find."

"You wanted them to find?"

"Of course. We all have to find some way of leaving our mark, don't we?"

He spins now, leering down, holding a velvet pouch in one hand, the cloth the deep maroon of blood clotted in a bruise. With a flourish, he unties the sash holding the pouch rolled and shakes it out for her inspection.

Held in loops and pockets of the pouch are the tools of his trade: "Needles, skewers, knives, studs, rings, metal molds for brandings." He unsnaps a compartment and withdraws a square foil packet. "Oh, and rubbers. I believe in safe sex."

Now he turns the pouch to his own speculation. "Let's see. What shall we start with?"

"Look," Anne moves warily, slowly rising to her feet, "why don't I go get us a couple more drinks, and we can—"

John uses one hand to push her down onto the couch. "And go out to the kitchen where the phone is? I don't think so."

"So you think I'm just going to sit here and let you do this?"

John selects an item from the pouch and holds it up before her, letting her see the scalpel's blade before he circles the couch. Once he's behind her, he leans down and gently, almost lovingly, begins to cut away the costly material of her right sleeve. She's paralyzed as the skin beneath is laid bare.

"Why not? The rest did. You'd be amazed. Oh, they'd struggle a little, scream. But, they didn't really fight back. Like they'd been conditioned to recognize the superior force and give in to it."

He finishes cutting and puts his face down tenderly next to hers. "Or, like they really did get off."

"Maybe I'm not like all the rest."

John chuckles as he starts around the couch again. When he reaches into his pants pocket for the surgical gloves, he responds, "How do you know all the rest of them didn't say that at first?"

Almost as if he senses her sudden urge to flee, he's on her, wrestling her down until he's on top, her breath crushed out of her, pinned beneath his weight. Once he's balanced there, he calmly reaches to his toolkit for the first needle.

"You're no different," he murmurs, sliding the needle tip so lightly along the skin of her vulnerable arm, "when you feel the first prick, see the blood bead up and trickle slowly down the needle, you'll scream and try to fight me. Then, I'll hit you again, only this time I'll knock out a few teeth, and after that, you'll take whatever I give."

Now he moves the needle up her neck to her face, causing her to inhale tightly. She manages to free one hand, and she tries to stop her fingers from shaking as she draws them down his arm.

"You know," she tries not to gasp, tries to entice him, "I think maybe this could be a turn-on."

John hesitates, intrigued, as she tries to move suggestively beneath him. "What if we go slow, so we can both get into it."

The hand stroking his arm attempts unobtrusively to push it back, but he suddenly reverses the hold, forcing her arm back down.

"I've got another idea: Why don't you decide where we should start?"

But he's already resting the needle on her cheek. She tries to turn away, unaware that she's only exposing herself more to him. She cries out, raw, as she feels the needle pierce the flesh, sliding in, blood spilling out—

—and then his hand begins to shake.

He releases the needle, blinking, and sits up, confused. He shakes the hand once, twice. But, when his whole upper body begins to weave, she ignores the pain and pushes up against him. He tumbles to one side of the couch like a rag doll, she wriggles out from beneath him, still trembling. She slides to the floor, weak at first, but regaining control with each passing second.

"About fucking time. I've gotta find something that'll work faster from now on."

John, slumped against the couch, tries to command his failing muscles to carry him up, but he only succeeds in staggering a few feet to a side table, where he loses his balance and crashes heavily to the floor.

"The drink..." is all he can splutter.

Anne's fingers probe her face and find the needle still impaling the skin there, blood streaking freely. When she turns to him, her face is almost as distorted as his sideways vision, from pain and rage. Her voice is a hoarse shriek, "You son-of-a-bitch! What did you do to me?"

She pulls the needle out and stares at it—or more specifically, at the blood. When he groans lightly behind her, she whirls and plants a firm kick in his chest. He cries out, testament to his still-active nervous system.

"Yeah, asshole, a muscle relaxant. They use it mainly on horses. A veterinarian friend of mine got it for me. She thinks I get off on it." Then, with a giggle, she adds, "She's not so far off the mark."

John struggles, limp, to an all-fours position, and Anne kneels beside him, fascinated. "See, it's perfect. It'll leave you feeling pain."

She runs the tip of the needle along the skin of his unsteady face, resting the tip against his cheek in precisely the same place where he pierced her. She holds this for a moment, relishing the terror in his eyes, then pulls her hand back.

"But you just won't be able to move. You probably just thought that weird taste was the generic vodka, I'll bet."

He lunges—although it might be more correct to say he lets himself fall—at her, and she jumps back easily, laughing as he smashes against the couch. He winds up with head and back propped clumsily against the bottom, legs splayed out on the floor.

He musters as much bravado as he can for a final threat. "Don't fuck with me, bitch...," is what he means to say, but somehow what comes out sounds more like, "Do fu wi me, bi..."

Anne laughs like a child delighted by the antics of a ridiculous clown. "Oh, stop."

Then, she feels the blood drip off her chin, and her mood abruptly shifts. She wipes an angry hand across her face, spreading crimson.

"Don't you want to know how I knew about you? Huh?" She drops down next to him; only his eyes move in response. "This is the best part: I didn't. We're just...strangers in the night."

John can barely force words out of his deadened lips now, although his mind is racing behind his dilated eyes. "You mean..."

She steps away, lithe, to pick up his toolkit with interest. "That's right. I gave you the drink before you tried anything, didn't I? Maybe that's because—" she pauses to draw forth the scalpel, "—I'm just like you, and neither of us knew it."

Then she reconsiders. "No, wait a minute. I'm not like you, because I would never be so deluded as to think you might get off on what I'm gonna do to you. You really believe that, don't you?"

Anne kneels beside him, running one hand dreamily along the rasping skin of his chest, the other hand still holding the open blade. "And you're all the same, too."

"Wha'...wha' are you goin' do?"

She leans down to kiss him, and John feels that, too; but he can't take his eyes off the hand circling his crotch—the hand with the blade.

"You think," she begins, moving her lips down his throat to his shoulders and chest, "that women actually enjoy being subjected to your sweat and your ramming and your cum. Don't you? Just like my daddy. But, the truth is that you're only necessary to propagate the species. When we can do that without you, we will. Believe me."

She raises her head to see his reaction, and she sees his bulging eyes fixed on the knife.

"What are you goin' do?" he shouts.

She kisses his pierced nipple, the taste of metal cold on her tongue; and the knife point rests on his shrunken crotch. She smiles, considering, prolonging the moment, his fear—

—and without warning she takes the ring penetrating the nipple in her mouth and jerks her head back, tearing the ring through the sensitive flesh.

John cries out, as much in surprise as pain.

She smiles at him, the gruesome ring still held in her teeth, then spits it aside. She abandons the scalpel, takes one of his inert arms, and peels the glove off to try on her own hand, smoothing it on sensuously.

"Maybe I'll give you a taste…" she starts, then trails off at a new thought. "Look at it this way: It takes most couples ten, twenty years to find out the truth about each other. But we already know the truth, don't we? That there's no such thing any more as safe sex. And there are worse ways to die—much worse ways—than from some disease."

John, still panting in agony, groans, a sound of pure despair that pulls her from her reverie. She shucks the contemplative mood like an old skin, turning happily to his toolkit.

"I'd use my own, but I'd have to go back into the kitchen, and I'd rather not, with Kenny there and all."

"Kenny?" John croaks.

"Yeah. That smell? Kenny. All six pieces of him." Then, she remembers, and giggles. "Make that seven."

Anne begins matter-of-factly pulling needles from the pouch, examining each with an experienced eye and a slow simmering of rage.

"And, I'll tell you something else, sweetheart: they'll never catch me, because I don't want a headline. I just wanna pay you back and then get rid of you. Every one of you."

She pulls the other glove off him and onto herself. "And look what I got this time out—how lucky can a little girl be? Let's see. What shall we start with?"

She selects a long, thick implement, then straddles him, bending close.

His cries echo for a long time through the tastefully decorated living room.

♦

Lisa Morton is a screenwriter, Halloween expert, and the author of dozens of works of short fiction. She is a three-time winner of the Bram Stoker Award (for the short story "Tested", the novella The Lucid Dreaming, and the non-fiction book *A Hallowe'en Anthology*), and she is also a recipient of the Black Quill Award (for editing the anthology *Midnight Walk*). Her first novel *The Castle of Los Angeles* was recently nominated for the Black Quill Award, and her second novella, *The Samhanach*, was published for Halloween 2010 by Bad Moon Books.

www.lisamorton.com

"A Speck in the Universe"

by Ripley Patton

Freshmen are notorious for chasing alien pussy, and I was no exception. Everyone who knew me—my netschool teacher, my parents, my older sibs—warned me against it. Even my gravball coach said, "Don't be an idiot, boy. That alien snatch has been all over the universe." During Uni orientation they made us sit through an educational mindvid about the dangers and reproductive frustrations of interplanetary intercourse. Don't they know all that negative hype just makes us want to go there even more? What nineteen-year-old, newly unfettered by the constraints and conventions of his home planet, wouldn't jump at the chance of making it with a female of a completely different species?

I chose a Rontooi because they look like earth women, except they are blue, have gills and, rumor has it, they never put out. Now there's a challenge: every one a beautiful, azure, long-haired virgin ripe for the picking. The day after orientation I asked one out. She was a junior and her name was Yonnie. She was totally into me.

It was your typical college romance. We went to the net bar and whispered our passwords into each other's ears. We watched virtual porn from tandem headsets our limbs entwined. We spent hours in each other's dorm rooms making out and ignoring our friends. Occasionally, we went to class together. Mostly we just watched the webcast version late at night and laughed at our professor's quirky maturities. And she never put out.

I tried every trick known to undergraduate man. I tried the traditional "slow and steady" working my way in sweaty increments toward that last line of intimacy. When that didn't work I broke up with her three times, hoping for desperate broken-hearted sex or, better yet, makeup sex. I played the bad boy telling her I was no good for her; I'd ruin her. That usually works. Women seem to think sex is a quick dose of redemption. But not Yonnie. I faked illness and injury but received no sympathy sex. I did another girl and let it slip, hoping that jealousy might be the ticket, but Yonnie just smiled and shrugged. I was even desperate enough to try the new date drug, Lazerjuice, in her drink one night. I found out that the only effect it has on a Rontooi is to cause excessive flatulence, which did nothing to further my cause that night.

One evening, two weeks before Spring Break, at the bitter end of a particularly hopeful make-out session, I lost my cool and called her a nasty name. It was a racial slur I'd heard used for the Rontooi that, at that moment, was so appropriate it exploded from my aching lips, "Blue-baller bitch!"

She pulled away from me, stood up and her mouth gaped. Before I could collect even a lame apology she asked, "Why do you call me this Charlu? (My name is Charles but she calls me Charlu.) I began a brief and faltering explanation of the cause, color and condition of my testicles. To my utter astonishment, she demanded visual proof.

"Let me see this coloring. I did not know this about earth men."

So, I showed her. She looked right past my impressive manhood and smiled at my bluish balls like women look at cute babies that aren't theirs. That seemed somewhat hopeful.

"What color is usual?" she asked as I zipped up carefully.

"Pink, I guess."

"Too bad," she said laughing as she sat back down across from me. "Charlu, these balls of yours," and she gestured at my crotch, "It is not why Rontooi are called blue-ballers. Our naming has nothing to do with earthmen's anatomy." Then she gently and firmly took my hands in hers, looked earnestly in my face and said, "Your appendage is but a speck in the universe." Then she left me.

♦ You can imagine my surprise when two days later she stopped by my room to invite me to her homeworld for Spring Break. I was skeptical.

"But didn't we break up the day I showed you my balls?"

"Did you wish to break up again?" she asked puzzled.

"Never mind," I covered myself brilliantly. "I'd love to come with you." I knew full well the legends of Rontoo, a huge wet planet where the natives live in spinning communes and have ongoing orgies. Maybe Rontooi only made it on Rontoo. Here was the invitation I'd been waiting for. Never in my wettest dreams had a private showing of my bluing nads paid off so well.

♦ It wasn't until the second shuttle layover on route to Rontoo that I realized my girlfriend intended to educate me. She began with Rontooi biology 101. Male Rontooi, much like male earthlings, have an endless supply of raw reproductive material. The females, however, have only one egg per lifetime. Their first mating stimulates the emergence of the egg for fertilization. This one egg will be a Rontooi woman's only offspring and it is never wasted on the likes of me. It would go unfertilized by my incompatible sperm, shrivel up and die. On this she spared no detail. I gathered that her egg was to be fertilized during our Spring Break visit by some virile Rontooi male.

"What about afterward?" I pressed her. "Once your egg has been used aren't you free to mate as much as you want?" It wasn't as good as my virgin alien fantasy, but it would do.

"Then I give myself away," she said simply. It sounded good to me.

♦ The Rontooi fertilization ceremony occurred on our last day there. By then I was desperate for something sensational. Don't get me wrong; Rontoo is pleasant enough if you like swimming through beautiful mansions of corral filled with naked blue women who never put out. For me it was the same old torture, just wetter. We ate a lot of exotic seafood and I learned several new water sports. Thankfully, I didn't have to meet Yonnie's parents. Rontooi are raised by the commune without knowledge of their progenitors. I did get to meet "The Fertilizer". His name was Naten. He was huge with navy dread locks. He was hung like a walrus and his balls were a deep sapphire. I was glad I had maintained my Earthly modesty and worn my Speedo.

On the last day I watched him swim away with Yonnie to begin preparations for what I hoped would be the long awaited Rontooi orgy. Yonnie turned back to say goodbye and I shooed her into the distance. All my efforts were finally going to pay off.

Three hours later I was led above sea level and outside onto a massive circular deck that seemed to melt into the ocean surrounding it. A large pool was inset in the very center. Polished glass bleachers, like smooth rainbow-colored icebergs, ascended steeply, all around it filled with smiling, chattering Rontooi. The entire commune was decked out in their best swim wear and children rode the shoulders of their favorite housemates.

I was taken to a seat thoughtfully reserved for me, about half way up, with a perfect view into the pool. Yonnie was naked and immersed in the center. Her arms and legs were spread wide and strapped with stretchy cord to four clasps at the edge of the pool. Her eyes were closed and she looked peaceful or asleep. She had never been more beautiful to me, and I could hardly wait my turn.

The crowd fell silent at some cue I had missed and then Rontooian music, something like whales doing Karaoke, came from somewhere. I didn't see a band so it must have been piped in.

I noticed that the pool had begun to spin slowly. Yonnie's hair drifted like blue kelp across her face and over her aqua nipples. She was a siren and I, a poor drooling sailor stuck on shore. The music and spinning increased in tempo, faster and faster, until Yonnie was only a blue smear-like eye in the apex of a raging whirlpool. Then Naten approached the side of the pool in something like a terry cloth bathrobe. He stood with his back to my side of the crowd and dramatically threw off the robe flexing his hard cerulean ass. I thought it was a little much, but the crowd went wild. He stayed poised, at the very edge of the pool, for a long time doing nothing that I could see as Yonnie spun faster and faster. So much for Rontooi foreplay. And then he dove, with perfect form, directly into the center of the pool where I knew Yonnie was tied. I cried out, expecting to hear the sound of their bodies colliding. I thought surely he had crushed her or broken her ribs diving head first into her like that but the crowd sat raptly waiting, unalarmed. The spinning continued and nothing changed for several minutes except the blue blur in the middle of the pool grew larger.

Finally, a small blue hand emerged from the swirling apex and the crowd cheered. It wasn't just a hand, though; it was a blue ball about the size of a babies head with this little hand rising out of it. Two more hands emerged but they were bigger and they held the ball up together and presented it for everyone to see. Then up came Yonnie and Naten grinning from ear to ear. It was they who held the ball that wasn't a ball at all. It was a Rontooi egg—Yonnie's successfully fertilized egg and their future child. Naten climbed gracefully from the pool and Yonnie handed the egg to him with the look women give cute babies that *are* theirs. Her eyes searched the crowd until she found me and she gave me a dazzling smile, a smile of promise. Naten cradled the egg proudly and the crowd left their seats and swarmed him, blocking my view of that dripping goddess in the pool. I fought my way to Naten and on past, trying to get to Yonnie. By the time I reached the pool's rim the spinning water had slowed and she was nowhere to be seen. I turned and called her name several times over the crowd, thinking she was swarmed by them as well and would make her way to me if she knew where I was. Naten broke through his admirers and came to my side.

"Yonnie is not here," he said, holding the egg out to me. Its little hand reached toward me and I jumped back in alarm.

"Where is she then?" I asked, thinking she at least could have told me she had more to do while I waited, once again, for the prize I had worked so hard for.

"She has given herself up," said Naten.

"Yes, with *you*. I saw all that! What about me?" I heard myself whining and finished assertively, "She's going to be with me now." Naten looked truly concerned.

"Charlu, Yonnie is no more. She is in the water."

"She isn't in the water. Naten, we're right here. Do you see her?" We were both standing at the edge of the pool which was obviously empty. I was beyond frustrated.

I saw a sea of worried faces behind Naten. Someone took the ball-baby gently from him. He took my left arm in his firm grip and said, "She is in the water, though we cannot see her. It is difficult to explain in your words. You might say she is 'dissolved'."

"Dissolved?" I repeated dumbly.

"All Rontooi females liquefy after mating. They give themselves away for the egg."

The pool had stopped spinning. Only a gentle ripple played across the water and the blue smear was gone. Yonnie was gone.

♦ Some smooth-skinned, old Rontooi explained it to me later on my trip to the shuttle launch. A one-handed egg, like Yonnie's, is apparently a bouncing baby boy. A multi-handed egg is female and will eventually split into as many girl baby balls as hands it once sported. I didn't ask how many hands are possible because I didn't want to know. The egg, however many hands it starts with, is put back in the pool where it swims and grows and thrives (and if it's female, divides) all the while absorbing the nutrient-rich juices that were once its mother. The infants are like tadpoles that, in about six months, will develop arms and legs and a head and walk out of that pool ready for solid food and a lap to sit on. Apparently, that's why the Rontooi are called blue-ballers; they all start out as a little blue ball with a hand sticking out. It seems to me that the other reason still applies just as well.

You might think I'd be angry after all I've been through. All that time I wasted wooing her and an entire college semester lost single-handedly "nursing" my poor blue balls. I should probably be bitter, but I'm not. Maybe it was some kind of sick Rontooi prank on the horny earthman. Maybe she was an alien tease and I was just her freshman boy toy. I like to think she wasn't that shallow. I like to think she cared about me as a person. Mostly though, I think about what it would have been like to finally "do her" just to see her dissolve in a blue puddle at my feet.

Thank God I escaped her clutches just in time. That kind of thing could scar a guy's libido forever.

♦

Ripley Patton is an American happily living on the South Island of New Zealand where she writes short speculative fiction, flash, and whatever else strikes her fancy. She is a three-time nominee of the Sir Julius Vogel Awards, and her story "Corrigan's Exchange" won the SJV for Best Short Story in 2009.

She is also the founder and President of SpecFicNZ, the national writers association for speculative fiction writers in and from New Zealand.

Ripley is currently working on her first novel, a YA contemporary fantasy.

www.ripleypatton.com
rippatton.livejournal.com

"The Salt Line"

by Grant Stone

The bus squealed to a stop. The doors hissed open as I stowed the comic book in my bag. Dad was already out of his seat, blocking the aisle, trying to wrench his backpack out of the netting. He moved back a little and I took the gap and jumped down without touching the steps. My feet crunched on gravel.

Apart from the bus, the carpark was deserted.

I had seen a hawk circling, back before we left the main road, an hour ago. Since then we'd passed fields, some of them still green, if overgrown, but there had been no traces of livestock. The engine died with a cough.

I leaned against the Department of Conservation sign and watched the others disembark. The bus couldn't have been more than half full - there was nobody else my age. Nobody had looked like they were enjoying it, especially the last half hour, crawling up and down hills with dust creeping through the windows and under the door.

A man in a brown tweed suit climbed down the steps. He had the look of a maths teacher and carried a walking stick, although he didn't seem to need it. He offered his arm to help a silver-haired woman down.

The next two off the bus were soldiers. You'd be able to tell just by the curve of their shoulders and their straight backs, even if they weren't wearing their dress fatigues.

The driver opened the luggage hatch and retrieved a collapsible wheelchair. With the assistance of one of the soldiers he helped a very elderly man down the steps. The soldiers made a real fuss over him, put a rug over his knees and adjusted his beret.

A woman in a white dress and sunhat stood in the doorway and squinted into the sky. Dad was right behind her, stuck. He polished his glasses on the corner of his shirt and waited.

I heard footsteps on the path. The man walking up to greet us looked the picture of health, in boots and shorts and cotton shirt, at least until he got close. Then I could see his left eye was white as sand and the last two fingers on his right hand were missing. He was frowning but when he saw me he gave me a wink and grinned.

The other passengers remained clumped together in the middle of the car park.

'Haere Mai,' he said, 'Welcome all. I trust you had a good trip. I'm Paul and I'll be your guide today. You're nearly at the line—just a gentle walk and we'll be there. But we don't need to head off just yet. You need a few minutes to shake the dust off.' The elderly woman hadn't waited—while Paul had been talking she'd pulled a tiny table and folding chairs from somewhere. The maths teacher was pouring her a mug of tea from a tartan thermos. 'Also, if you've got any questions, now's a good time to ask them.'

A hand emerged from the back of the crowd.

'Yes.'

'Will it be possible to take pictures?'

Paul smiled. 'No problem at all. The funny thing is though, once people get up there they tend to forget to take them. I should warn you. You've all seen pictures, seen it on television. It's a little more intimidating when you see it up close. There's plenty of seating up there if you feel faint. If you have any difficulties whatsoever, let me know. And don't feel bad if you want to turn back before we reach it. It's perfectly natural.'

One of the soldiers snorted. 'That's the last thing it is.'

♦ While the others unpacked sandwiches and clustered in whispering knots, I walked across to the far side of the carpark. We had to be more than a little walk away. The path disappeared into brush, but where it should have been visible above the treeline there was just an infinite blue.

Dad walked over and handed me a sandwich. 'Ready little man?'

'Sure.'

'Beautiful day for a tramp. Your mum and I used to come up here all the time. Well,' he waved his hand, 'further up north. You know, before.'

A couple of weeks ago in History class, Sam had leaned over to me. *Know what the worst word in the English language is*, he whispered.

What?

Before.

♦ The others put away their lunch and wandered over to the path. It was pretty narrow, so we formed a line. Dad and I were last. The light dimmed almost immediately as we walked into the bush. Sun dripped through in patches and made the leaves sparkle.

I jogged up to the front. The woman in the sunhat giggled as I went past.

'Day off school?' Paul asked.

'Two. We came up from Christchurch yesterday.'

He nodded. I'm from Christchurch, myself. Haven't been back since it became the capital. Crusaders still winning?'

I shrugged.

'Not many your age come up to see it. You're what, thirteen?' I nodded. 'Don't blame you. You were still in nappies when it happened.'

'What happened to your hand?'

He looked at the white line that marked the end of his hand where his fingers should be, as if he was seeing it for the first time. 'Got too close.'

'And your eye?'

'Got too close,' he said.

Twenty minutes later the path opened into a large clearing. A DOC hut took up most of the space and there were a few picnic tables scattered about.

'Nearly there folks,' Paul said, 'We'll rest here for a few minutes to let you catch your breath. There are some displays set up in the hut if you're interested, or if you'd just like to get out of the sun.'

Dad fished a couple of bottles of water from his backpack and they were still pretty cold. I put my finger to the glass and traced a wavy line in the moisture, drew a crude ship above it and a circle-lines happy sun. My father coughed and I brushed the picture away before he could see.

'What time is it?'

Dad looked at his watch. 'Ten thirty.'

Any other Wednesday I'd be standing outside Mr. Emerson's room. That's where they'd all be now, socks pulled up, single file. Mr. Emerson had been pulled out of retirement after it happened. *Perfect for teaching history, he is,* Sam had said, *seen so much of it.*

'Want to go look?' Dad asked.

I shook my head.

'Suit yourself,' he said and wandered over by himself.

I figured Paul had called another rest for the elderly couple, but they were fine. The guy had taken off his jacket and slung it over his shoulder and was laughing at something. The soldier who'd been pushing the wheelchair didn't look so good. He was hunched over, sweat dripping off him. The wheelchair had thin, solid tyres that didn't roll very well on the dirt track.

Dad came back and sat down again, a strange expression on his face.

'Any good?'

He shook his head. 'Nothing much. Big map of the South Island, showing where the line is. A few photos.' His voice dropped to a whisper. 'A list'. He didn't need to say more. A list of the dead. Or rather, a list of those confirmed dead by whoever had the job of figuring it out. A black wall covered in names circled Cathedral Square, then snaked all the way down to the Arts Centre. They were still building it. Dad got worked up whenever we passed it, reckoned it was a bloody useless waste of time.

Mum's name wasn't on it.

♦ Dad had told me about it when he figured I was old enough. 'You have to understand that she always loved you,' he said and took off his glasses, rubbed the bridge of his nose, 'It wasn't her fault. Things were—crazy. People would go off, not be seen again.' He shrugged, as if it could have been worse. I knew it could have. Ross Johnson's grandparents had chugged a bottle of sleeping pills and gone out to the garden, to sit

81

in deckchairs and wait. 'Maybe she thought there was something she could do. You know how she was.'

Mum was awesome. Most families have a portrait on the wall, or an aging wedding photo. We had a copy of the front page of the Press, showing Mum being carted off by police, along with a bunch of other protestors. That was how they'd met — pushed together in the back of a paddy wagon.

Then one day the police called and Dad took the bus over to Lyttleton. The car was unlocked, keys still in the glovebox. At first he wondered if she'd just jumped in, but he knew she'd never do that. It was the next day, when Rawiri's wife called, then uncle Martin, that it all came together. Rawiri and uncle Brett had gone the same night. I imagined Mum driving over for uncle Brett first, over in Hornby, pulling up outside, lights off, keeping the engine as quiet as she could. Then across to Cashmere for Rawiri. He'd been in the picture from the Press too, arms twisted up behind his back, policeman hissing in his ear. They'd stolen a Zodiac and gone, straight out to sea, straight out to the line.

I sloshed the last of the water around the bottle. I could imagine them, Mum in the thermal dive gear left over from her time with Greenpeace, crouched in the back of the boat, her unqueued grey hair flying out behind, hand on the throttle of the outboard.

I tried to figure it out, once. Phoned up some boat shops to try and find out how far a Zodiac could run. One tank of gas or was it likely they'd have two? How far was the line, anyway? Back then there wasn't a lot of information and if a kid asked—they were trying to protect us, I guess. After a while I realised I didn't want to know if she'd made it all the way.

♦ We were at the front of the line now. Dad bothered Paul with questions and he answered without taking his eyes off the track ahead.

'Where are all the birds?'

'South. Won't come near the place. It's not just birds, either. No animals here now. Dig all day and you'll never find a worm'

'That can't be good for the trees.'

'It's not. The Rata won't spread without birds. Not long, maybe fifty years, all this will be gone, it'll be all gorse or sand. It's the same out in the ocean. Half a kilometre from the line there's just nothing.'

Dad snorted. 'Bad for fishing.'

'Yep.'

The trees still looked pretty good to me, rough and solid and alive. It was weird to think of them gone. It was cool and green here, but silent. No animals here, not even an ant. We may as well have been on the moon.

'Will it spread?'

'Not as far as we can tell. The land along the line will be a desert, but there's no indication the line is going to shift.'

'There was no indication something like the line could ever exist. Until it did.'

'Yeah.' Paul rubbed the back of his neck. 'Don't make any long term plans.'

♦ We stopped after another fifteen minutes. It had been growing steadily more dark and I realised I hadn't seen even a gap in the leaves for some time.

Paul's voice was hushed. 'We're here.'

I could hear someone praying behind me. The whole group was close together now, huddling in the dark.

'OK,' Paul said, and walked on, not the same way he'd marched up the track. His footsteps were careful now, like he was creeping past a sleeping beast.

Dad squeezed my hand and I didn't let go. We turned the corner.

At first it wasn't so bad. A few rows of seats. A solid waist-high fence and then the line itself. It could have been a cinema screen. But it was the black of the void and it went up, and out, further than I could see. It went up forever.

My stomach turned over. Dad fumbled for the nearest seats and pulled us down. I put my head between my knees, looked down at my shoes and tried to remember the blue sky at the other end of the trail.

I could hear the reactions of the others as they saw it for the first time, their sharply indrawn breaths.

One of the soldiers lost it, started shouting, swearing. 'It's OK, mate,' the other soldier said, and I heard a pounding sound. 'It's OK,' he said again, his voice was muffled. I looked around. His shoulders stuttered up and down as he sobbed.

♦ After a few minutes I looked at the line again. Through the gaps in the fence, I could see the part where the land simply stopped, as if someone had taken a razor and cut the world. Beyond that was nothing. No stars. No wind. A nothing so pure it pressed on my eyes like a block of obsidian. The rest of the world could have been right on the other side of the line. Or maybe the whole universe had been broken into shards like glass dropped on concrete. Or maybe it was all just gone. The void answered nothing.

The last of the cries stopped. We were all sitting now, silent.

The soldiers walked down to the front and stopped just before the fence, set their legs wide. 'Ka mate' the taller one shouted and they slapped their palms on their thighs. The haka took up the space, boomed around the clearing. I kept time, pounding my fist against the seat.

'Hūpane! Hūpane! Hūpane! Kaupane! Whiti te rā!'

One last upward step! Then step forth! Into the sun that shines!

They shouted a final 'He,' and instantly the silence fell again.

The elderly captain gripped the arms of his wheelchair and began to sing in a high and uncertain voice. 'Eternal Father, strong to save, whose arm hath bound the restless wave,'

We all joined in including Dad. I don't think he'd ever been inside a church in his life.

'For those in peril...' I didn't know the words, but after a while I figured out the melody and hummed. The hymn faded out in the middle of the second verse.

Just in front of the line was a white substance, crusted and collected the length of the clearing like a spine laid on the ground. The crystals sparkled from some unknown light and it wasn't until I felt Paul's hand on my chest that I noticed I'd walked all the way down to the front.

'Don't get too close,' he said.

'What is that stuff?'

'We call it salt, but nobody knows. Some people though—it's like it calls to them. That's why we have the fence,' he said, and rubbed the scar line of his missing fingers.

I walked with Paul back to where Dad was sitting.

'What are you doing running off mate,' he said, trying for a jokey feel, but his voice quivered and his eyes were wet. People were already starting back up the trail in ones and twos. Nobody wanted to stay.

Dad kept his arm tight around my shoulders the whole way back.

I wondered if Mum had felt it too, the pull of the salt. If it had called to her, all the way over in Riccarton, got her out of bed and into the car, her hands turning the ignition, got her to round up the old crew and drive to Lyttleton, find a boat, cut the mooring rope. I wondered if it would call for me again one day. Then we emerged from under the canopy and the light was like mercury and the sun was sweet on my face.

♦

Grant Stone hails from Auckland, New Zealand. His fiction has appeared in *Shimmer, Andromeda Spaceways Inflight Magazine, Semaphore* and *Prima Storia*. He has been known to blog on occasion.

d1sc0r0b0t.blogspot.com

"I Feel Lucky"

by SatyrPhil Brucato

She was my girlfriend once, y'know. Before the brawls and black leather, she called herself Linda and lived with me for about two years. No, that wasn't really her name and I knew it even then. People got reasons for their secrets, though, and I respected that much. She never gave me reason to ask till after she left, and by then... well, you know the rest as well as anyone.

I'm still not sure why she took the path she chose, but I recall the girl she was back then. Haunted but sweet, so much so that it made my heart hurt sometimes just to look at her. Linda was always a big girl—not fat, never, but tall and strong-shouldered. She had a softness to her that you'd never guess to see her now. That sharp look you see on the news... no, that wasn't my girl. I guess there was a ghost of that running 'round in her long before we met, and I guess it kinda won in the end. For a while, though, she had a tender side. Sometimes I think about going after her and seeing how much of it—if any—is still alive in there.

Oh, hey, that reminds me—hang onto this for me, will you? Thanks.

You'd never know from those combat clodhoppers she wears now, but she loved to go barefoot. When we went walking, she'd just amble along like some shoeless hippie. Seemed like she was testing herself sometimes, walking on gravel and blacktop hot enough to fry eggs on. Said it made her feel alive. That should've told me something but I just thought it was cute back then.

We met in Charlie's, back before the Scotts took over. It was a high fine blues joint back then, all wood and beer-sticky tables. I was there with Matt and Chris and Marty, checking out the Wednesday open-mike. Place was packed, on account of Julie Penn and Cheryl Mack. The fans were going but the place was thick with sweat and smoke. I was propped up against the bar and Linda was standing nearby, and both of us kept shifting aside to let people pass by. Even then, she had her shoes off. "You're gonna get stepped on," I said. I think I was smiling.

"Oh, yeah, like that'd be something new." She grinned when she said it, but there were broken-glass edges in that smile. Her voice was clipped, her eyes wary. Challenging. I think that's why I kept talking. I never did like skittish girls.

We wound up sparring all night, like Hepburn and Tracy in a blues bar. She was smart. I wasn't bad, either. She bought me drinks, refused to let me return the favor. Even then, her actions said don't own me. She was good at being owed, but never good with debt.

Speaking of drinks, you up for another round?

We kissed in the parking lot that night. It was weird. We looked at each other for a long time when I stopped by my car. She refused to let me walk her to hers. The streetlights caught her eyes, made 'em shine. We stopped breathing, I think. I leaned in a little. She never closed her eyes, so I did it for both of us.

Next thing I know, she's got me shoved up against my car. Hard. Strong. Her fingers are in my hair. There's Jack Daniels in my mouth. Hungry lips on mine. Teeth. Damn! I'm not sure if or when I started breathing, but we'd been there a while by that time. Suddenly, she jerked back away from me. Shook her head. "Oh, yeah," she said to herself. Shook it again. Nodded. "Oh yeah, oh yeah, oh yeah." She picked up her shoes, then. Smiled kinda shyly. "Give me a call, huh?" I think I nodded. She walked off fast, like she was trying to get away.

She moved in three months later. The getaway came two years after that.

Yeah, she was always strong. Not like some of 'em, you know, flipping-over-cars strong. But she was a lot stronger than me, even back then. I gotta admit, and don't take this the wrong way, but I liked that. Some girls, you've gotta be careful you don't break 'em. With Linda, she was the one being careful. That first few times we made love—and yeah, it was love we were makin' then—she broke stuff. Three ribs. My nose. My dresser. Heh. Remember when I had that cast on my wrist? It wasn't stairs that did that. I've still got scars down my back from... well, that was a long time ago. Good thing I had good medical insurance—heh! And fast. Damn, she was quick. I had to slow down for the both of us. I don't know, sometimes, what she saw in me then. I mean, she could have worn down a football team. But she seemed satisfied with me.

Yeah, it is a new jacket. Nice, huh? I should have bought me one of these years ago.

Linda loved country music. Can you imagine? She had a thing for Lyle Lovette—thought he was cute. And she could sing every Trisha Yearwood song. Linda used to say that Mary Chapin's "I Feel Lucky" was her personal theme song. I think she was joking. She'd put on Rosanne Cash and cry. In bed sometimes she'd sing "City of New Orleans" when she thought I was asleep. One day, I found her listening to "Blood and Fire" with wild eyes and a throat too full to speak. Seeing those eyes, all tears and unscreamed things, I wanted to hold her, yet run far away at the same time. She sensed that hesitation and slammed the door so hard the wall cracked. Not long afterward, she left.

Maybe if I'd reached out she'd still be here with me.

I don't know what made her that way. She had nightmares all the time, but never talked about 'em with me. I'd just hold her then, tight as I could. Run my fingers through her hair. Talk soft, like to a spooked horse. Stare into the dark and wish I could just take it all away from her. There wasn't any of that "It's just your imagination" shit between us, not even at four AM. I wouldn't have insulted her that way. Whatever happened, it was real and it was bad and it still had bits buried deep inside of her. I think she's still trying to rip 'em out, even now.

I think that's why she does what she does.

Reporters know nothing. She's no sadist. She doesn't like to hurt people... except maybe certain people. Every time she'd hurt me, she'd cry and say I'msorryI'msorryI'msorry over and over and over again. Linda had soft fingertips and gentle lips and... aw, hell, I don't wanna go there. But they're stupid and they're wrong. And I need another drink.

Heh.

We watched a lotta TV, she and I. Picture that: me and Riplash, curled up on a maroon love seat with a big mixing bowl full of popcorn, watching Seinfeld. Funny, huh? Butter breath, husks in our teeth. She wasn't Riplash then, just Linda. Big and beautiful with bed-head. Heh.

I wonder if she still remembers.

You can tell when someone's not there anymore. I mean, you can feel 'em when they're close by, even if you can't see 'em, and you know when they're not. You can feel an empty room, too, when it's really empty. Does that make sense? Me, I've become an expert on empty these last few years. I keep filling up the space and it just keeps feeling empty. I keep waiting for the sound of bare feet heavy on a hardwood floor. The creak of wood that means you're not alone. And yeah, I wake up sometimes with someone next to me, all warm and breathe-y. But they just feel like reruns. Songs I've heard too many times and that never meant that much to me the first time out. When they're gone, there's just dead air.

You're a good friend, dude. That's why I trust you with this.

Keep the key for me. I paid the rent for the next three months. After that, if I'm not back, you can have whatever you want from in there. Sell the rest, give it away, whatever. If I'm not back by September I won't be coming back. The bike's paid off, and I already took what I needed. Yeah, I should probably sober up first, I guess, but if I don't leave now I'm not gonna. And I can't stand another morning waking up to dead air.

Heh.

I don't expect she'll be around here much longer. Linda doesn't stay where she's not wanted. I wonder if she'll recognize when she is. Or if she's too far gone to care. So I wanna get on the road before she gets too far away. Right now, I have a good idea where she is. Tomorrow morning it'll be too late.

Gotta go, dude.

It's late.

But I feel lucky.

♦

SatyrPhil Brucato sold his first pro story to Marion Zimmer Bradley back in 1989. That tale—"Elynne Dragonchild" in *Sword & Sorceress IX*—became the first of many. Known throughout the 1990s as part of White Wolf's pack of leather-clad disreputables, Phil co-created the *Mage, Sorcerers Crusade, Changeling* and *Vampire: The Dark Ages* lines, contributing to over 80 books for that company.

In 2001, he founded Laughing Pan Productions, authoring *Deliria: Faerie Tales for a New Millennium*, and *Everyday Heroes* and *Goblin Markets* from 2003-2006. He's also been a steady columnist for *newWitch* magazine. His short stories have appeared in venues such as *Weird Tales* ("Ravenous") and *Bad-Ass Faeries 2* ("Loopholes").

Most recently, he co-edited the benefit anthology *Ravens in the Library* with his partner Sandra Buskirk. Satyr lives in Seattle now.

satyrblade.livejournal.com

"Ink Calls to Ink"

by Nathan Crowder

It was the scream which shook the soldier awake, and not the cold wind coming off the Thames. High, desperate, then cut short with a sound he could only describe as a meaty chomp. Old instincts came to the fore, and he raised the brim of his hat to scan the foggy Chelsea streets. Battersea Park was only dimly visible through the mid-morning murk, presenting the soldier with a shifting white canvas of indistinct shapes, and then nothing. No sign. Not even a random pedestrian passed by which the old soldier found unusual, even given the weather.

Adrenalin filled his veins for the first time in years. He listened intently for any sign of where the noise had come from. The turgid water of the river lapping below, and traffic on cobblestones far away, and there, just at the edge of his perception, a snuffling sound he hadn't heard since coming to London. Heavens no, he thought. Please don't let it be so. The sound of big paws with wicked black claws on the end approached the end of the alley nearest him. More than one, less than four, he thought. And though he quaked with fear, he kept the brim of his hat low so as not to be seen. He feigned sleep, hoping it would be enough. As the paws reached the end of the alley, they grew quiet. The soldier's eyes flickered in that direction, though he would not let his head signal his awareness.

He saw not animal, but instead, human feet—three sets of them. One large, definitely male. Another, was a thick-ankled woman, her strength evident in her gait.

The third set of feet belonged to a child, and although he found it hard to gauge age based on someone's feet, he took them to be close to twelve years of age. All were shoeless, despite the cold of the morning, though none of them seemed to notice. There were droplets of blood on their feet as well.

The three of them stood there, motionless, and the soldier felt their eyes burning into him. He didn't move, not even to breathe. And after an eternity, they turned and walked down the street. The soldier waited until he felt his muscles cramping before he moved again. Reaching for his crutch, he tossed back his long, ragged blue coat and struggled to stand. With only one leg, it was an ordeal at the best of times. Consumed by fear and still shaking as the adrenaline left his system, the task was somewhat more difficult. The soldier tucked his tin cup into his jacket and hobbled to the corner of the alley. He didn't need to go any further.

Some twenty feet down the narrow alley lay the corpse of a tiny woman. No more than two feet tall, she was anatomically perfect, or had been until she had been torn apart and partially consumed. Her still-perfect face stared at the one legged soldier with a look of glassy contempt. He felt her accusation settle deep into his gut. She couldn't have known he was right around the corner. And even if she had, the soldier knew she wouldn't have expected him to help. But still he recognized her and felt guilt for not doing something.

Thumbelina was an Anderson, after all, like the match girl, and the mermaid, and himself. Ink calls to ink. He thought long and hard, remembering his training. It had been so long ago and in an entirely other place. His eyes turned to the brick of the alley floor, and took in the bear prints. Three sets—one too big, one too small, and one—well, not just right, certainly. There was nothing right about this at all.

The steadfast soldier spun on his good leg and sped as fast as he could go through the streets of London, two thoughts burning in his mind.

"How did they get through?" And, "She will have to be told."

♦ It was late in the afternoon when the soldier found her. She was eating fish and chips from a cone of greasy newsprint a few blocks from her most recent squat. Finding Goldie was never particularly easy. Not unlike his fellow Ficts, she had no regular address. Many of the literary refugees, the Fictional Personae who had come to reside in London since the Kemzer-Lee Effect now lived on the streets or worse. Unlike the others, Goldie was not above breaking in to unused homes and making them her own until evicted by the police or homeowners. It was a delicate situation for the police. Sure, she was in clear violation of the law, but she wasn't entirely real, either.

It was true that she was flesh and blood now, and could easily pass for human. But she didn't have fingerprints, her hair would never grow longer, she would never get wrinkles, never grow old, and never die. Well, not naturally, at least. Thumbelina was more proof than the soldier would ever need that Ficts died just like anyone else when the chips were down.

Goldie was sitting on the railing overlooking the Thames right off Blackfriars, her curly blonde hair tied up in a Union Jack bandana. She had taken to wearing a Russian surplus army jacket, and black high-topped tennis shoes. No one walking by on the busy road was likely peg her has a Fict. To think—three years ago, she had only existed in children's story books. She had been one of the first to come over, and also one of the first to adapt. Not that any of their kind really adapted very much.

With no birth record, no school history, no work history, no real friends and contacts, and more than a little bit of culture shock, it had been impossible for the influx of Fictional Personae to integrate fully into society. They had appeared thanks to the dubious blessing of the Kemzer-Lee Effect and most were out on the street within a fortnight. England had been the first country to give them anything remotely like rights, perhaps because that was where the rift had opened. But even with those rights, it left them as second class citizens.

The soldier realized that Goldie had seen him coming, and didn't bother to hide his concern. She was not one of the Andersons. Her lineage traced back less than two hundred years to a writer named Southy. Very popular in England, the earliest stories painted her as an old woman, and then as Silver Hair.

It wasn't until 1904 that she was given the golden hair, but that was the image everyone remembered now. And when Doctors Erich Kemzer and David Lee switched on their quantum engine with the intent of creating free energy, they instead created an unintentional rift through which characters of fiction dripped like rarified wine. And when Goldie came through, it was this, more contemporary version which set her feet of ink upon England's fields of green. The science lads found closing the rift impossible. It was merely one of those things that, once done, is done.

There was no going back. And so Fictitious Personae entered the world, formed clans, and tried to blend in.

Oh, there were the spectacles and to-do's at first. The people all wanted to bask in the novelty of these well-remembered characters walking among them. Goldie had done the talk shows and even a cameo in a movie which went straight to DVD. And while the governments of the world scrambled with how to weaponize the rift and what to do with the Ficts, the people lived the fairy tale of meeting and getting to know these figures they had grown up with.

But the novelty wore off quickly. It turned out that growing up with an idealized image inevitably clashed with the reality of that character. Prince Charming was less charming once you saw him with spinach in his teeth, or getting drunk with the lads down at the pub. It made them human, and that was the worst thing they could be. People already gave less than two shits about most other humans, so one that aped a character from an old story was even easier to dismiss or even disdain. At least Goldie had experienced the fairy tale. By the time the steadfast soldier came, no one seemed to notice the Ficts any more, at least no more than they would the average bum on the street.

Goldie wiped her greasy fingers on the newsprint cone, transferring the ink to her fingers. "You have something to say to me, soldier? Spit it out. I don't have all day to sit around."

The steadfast soldier found his breath easily and his voice followed naturally thereafter. "The bears are in London."

Goldie's jaw turned to steel to match the intensity of her eyes. "You saw them?" The steadfast soldier could only nod in the fury of her gaze. "Show me where."

The soldier had already exhausted himself trying to find Goldie. With his one, old leg, the trip from Blackfriars to Battersea was not one he could take on foot again. Goldie flagged down a gypsy cab and pressed a wad of bills into the driver's hand as soon as they had piled into the back. The driver turned to her, looking her over from head to toe with blood-shot eyes. A cloud of ganja smoke curled around the red window fringe he had tacked into place. "Where to?"

"Chelsea, across from the Battersea Park," Goldie pointed to the handful of cash, "or as close as that will get us."

The soldier could not decide if tension was over having to spend hard-to-come-by money or the fact that the bears were in London. He wasn't sure how to broach the subject, and stayed wisely silent instead.

As the close London streets and speeding cars enveloped them, the two passengers let the sounds of the city keep them from speaking, Goldie lapsing into a sullen silence and the soldier into tired reflection. The bears coming to London spelled bad times for everyone, but it was inevitable that they would come through eventually. They hadn't been the first of the anthropomorphic Ficts to come across. One or two of the Aesop's trickled through now and again, and they were harmless enough. Then there was the incident with the Big Bad Wolf, of which the less said the better. The long and short of it was that just as Goldie and the soldier and the others had proven to be too human, the wolf and the others were too animal.

Goldie turned on the soldier in the cramped confines of the gypsy cab. "I don't understand how the bears could have gotten all the way into London without being noticed. You think someone would panic with a family of bears in the street."

"They can change."

This caused Goldie to raise a skeptical eyebrow. "Change? Change how?"

The soldier shrugged and looked out the window as the storefronts raced by. It was only his second time in a car, and he found himself enchanted by the experience. And anyway, his part in this was almost done. He could feel the shape of this, and he had no role in the confrontation. This had been a long time coming, this conflict between Goldie and the bears—centuries in the making. Once he put her on the trail, he could go back to the anonymity of street corner begging, dreaming of better times, of adventures he had lived, and of the beautiful but silent ballerina just always out of his reach. "They can look human. I can smell the difference, though, and you should be able to as well. And they don't have shoes. At least they didn't when I saw them. How do they change? I don't know. Maybe since they had a house, slept in beds, and ate porridge, they were already close enough to human that it was an easy transition. Does it matter?"

"It matters if I'm going to try and find them."

The soldier nodded, not looking at her. His voice was subdued, and he felt so tired. "Ink calls to ink. You'll find them. And then you'll kill them. And then there will be three less of us."

Goldie poked the soldier hard in the shoulder with a lead pipe she had removed from her coat. It got his attention—at least enough that he turned around and looked at her and the pipe before turning back to the window. Goldie snarled through clenched teeth. "They aren't like us. They aren't like us at all. They're animals."

The soldier didn't waste a look in her direction. "They lived in a house, slept in beds. They sound like people to me. You say they're animals. You know them best. Whatever. They killed Thumbelina, and they'll probably kill a lot more until someone stops them. But animals or not, they're still Fictionals. They don't belong here any less or any more than we do."

The interior of the cab grew silent again. Goldie clenched and unclenched her fist around the length of the pipe. She clenched and unclenched her teeth around words she couldn't find. The soldier could see her wanting to lash out, to strike the words out of his mouth, but it was too late. They were in her head now, and there was no denying it. Neither of them really belonged there. None of the Ficts did. And she was Goldilocks, who never really belonged anywhere if there was any truth to the stories. But at least here in London, there were no bears. Well, not until today.

The soldier's voice snapped her out of her reflection. "Have you ever wondered why all the Ficts are old timers like us? Why aren't there any comic book Fictional Personae?"

"Public domain," she answered quickly.

"What?"

"There's something called copyright. It's like a sacred seal. But it doesn't last forever, and while it's there, whoever created the characters owns them like slaves. But after a while, the characters earn their emancipation. We don't belong to the creator or his family or anyone anymore. We belong to the world. And once we belong to the world, we can be part of it."

Goldie turned to see the soldier staring slack-jawed at her. "How do you know that?"

She smiled grimly. "I don't. But it's as good an answer as any."

The cab screeched to a halt. "Meter's up. You be getting' out now."

"We aren't there yet." Goldie protested.

"You said as close as your money would get you. Here it is. Thank you. Have a nice day."

The soldier tugged on the sleeve of her coat. "It isn't far from here anyway. This is good enough."

Grumbling she followed the soldier from the cab. As it sped away, the soldier pointed down the narrow lane towards the still fog-shrouded Thames. "Head to the river, then three blocks to your left. You'll see the blood in the alley if the police haven't cordoned it off yet. There's something strange in the air today, so it's possible no one has seen Thumbelina but me. And I'm pretty sure no one will be able to track the bears like you, anyway."

Goldie sucked on her teeth, staring down the street. The soldier didn't like the look of steely contemplation in her eyes. He had seen it before, in the eyes of senior officers. "Don't sell yourself so short. You might be less than a whole man, but you can track them better than me."

The steadfast soldier swallowed hard. It was true, of course, and to see the affair through would be only right. But still…but still… "My part in this is done." He mumbled so low that only the stubble on his chin heard him. She propelled him into a slow, hopping step towards the river with a prod of her pipe.

The police had found the site, of course. One couldn't expect a murder to go unnoticed for too long in London, not even the murder of a Fict. The alley was cordoned off, with helmeted bobbies shooing away the gawkers and death-drawn rubber-neckers. The soldier led Goldie past the commotion, along the path he had seen the bears taking only a few scant hours before.

She had been right, no matter how much he hated to admit it. There, a few droplets of Fict blood on the concrete, and beyond, a fresh trio of scratches on a railing that could only have been left by claws. His tracking eye was good, his instincts flawless, and the transition of environment from the field to the city was not as off-putting as he had expected. The trail led down the street, through twisting alley, then over a short garden wall to the back of a quiet, brick two-story flat. He could smell them, their musk heavy on the air, as if... "They want us to find them."

Goldie grunted, and clambered atop the garden wall. She crouched there, her eyes narrowed to slits through which the blue of her irises sparked like inlaid sapphires. She didn't move for some time, watching the house quietly before lowering her hand to the soldier to help him up over the wall.

He had tracked them to the house. That was all she had wanted. But Goldie was not about to give up an ally, and he had grown tired of fighting it. This wasn't supposed to be his story, true. But he was a part of it now by virtue of him having found Thumbelina's body. The steadfast soldier considered that maybe his part would end the same as the tiny Fictional Personae, dead in an alley, mourned by none but the broken and lost of his kind. He took Goldie's offered hand and let her help him shimmy over the wall to the soft loam of the Chelsea flower garden. The golden-tressed Fict hopped down next to him, her pipe at the ready.

"How do we know they're still here?" he asked in hushed tones.

The smile Goldie gave as her only answer was cold and feral. It rattled the soldier. Stupid question, he thought. Of course she knows they were still there, waiting. It was a trap, after all. But knowing it was a trap didn't make it any less of a trap. The soldier had a hard time swallowing, his eyes turning from Goldie's smile to the black rectangle of the open back door several paces away. The darkness within seemed to roil with barely concealed menace, as if it were watching them.

She prodded him with her pipe. "You first. It's me they want, so they'll probably let you in without a fuss."

The soldier wet his suddenly dry lips with the flicker of a nervous tongue. He shifted awkwardly on his crutch in the soft dirt of the garden. "And what, pray tell, do you expect me to do when I'm in there? Limp on them?"

"Distract them." Her tone was flat, firm. There was no arguing with that voice. There was no point in her trying to fill him with false promises of safety. The bears had killed Thumbelina. There was no reason for them not to kill him too. But that would still give Goldie her distraction.

The soldier spit on the ground, the only defiance left in him. He was the steadfast soldier. He followed orders. It was what he did. Damned if Goldie didn't plan on exploiting that simple truth. Eyes brimming with hot, ink tears, he hobbled into the house with as much proud bearing as he could muster. When he was only one step into the house, his eyes had adjusted to the change of light.

And he saw the bears.

The youngest sat, so prim and proper at the kitchen table. The soldier blinked twice to see her as a bear, not as an urchin dressed in a clean but dated dress. One second, she was sitting drawing, with ribbons in her brown hair. The next second, the ribbons had been replaced with round, furry ears. Her forepaws were still stained the russet of Thumbelina's dried blood.

The other two bears were only terrifying shadows in his peripheral vision. Their scent, of musk and meat rotting between their powerful teeth, was overpowering. The snuffling of the two muzzles was strong enough to tug on his hair. The soldier paused mid-step, waiting for a powerful paw to swipe in and end his existence, but that blow did not come. He blinked, looking neither right nor left, and then continued into the home, taking a seat across from little bear.

The soldier realized that male and female bears sounded much the same when speaking, so it was impossible for him to tell who it was that addressed him from near the doorway. "We can smell her on you. And we thought we saw her at the wall. Where is she? Where is the little thief?"

"She was right behind me," the soldier mumbled. Then realizing that no one but the little bear heard him, he raised voice and said it again. But in his head, the words translated to, "I am her sacrifice. She cares nothing for me. I am forsaken." When he turned to look at the two, powerful brown bears, he did nothing to mask the fear on his face.

The bears lowered themselves to all fours and shuffled back and forth on their massive legs. Beyond them, the garden was clearly absent one golden-haired Fict. The steadfast soldier bit back the taste of bile that rose to the top of his throat. Mama Bear advanced on him with what looked to him like a reluctant gait, as if she was sorry for what she was about to do. Papa Bear shook his head in disgust and took two lumbering steps out the back door.

A shadow descended from on high, and death was upon Papa Bear in an instant as Goldie dropped from somewhere above the door, snapping his neck with one swift blow of her pipe. The suddenness of the action almost made the soldier yelp with surprise, but he was so numb with fear that he was virtually unresponsive. The sound of the blow, and of the enormous bear thumping to the ground was more than enough to get Mama Bear's attention, and she spun away from the threatened soldier with a roar of unrelenting rage.

With the doorway restricted by the body of her husband, the widowed bear found getting out into the garden virtually impossible. Reluctant to clamber across the corpse of her husband, she paced angrily, and then stood on her hind legs, torn between remorse and the needs for revenge. The soldier looked out past her restless, angry form, and could just barely see Goldie, proudly grinning above her recent kill. Goldie snorted and hawked, and spit dismissively onto the corpse of Papa Bear.

"No! Stop that you monster!" Mama Bear shouted, raged and roared.

The steadfast soldier felt himself achingly echoing the sentiment. They had killed his friend, true, and he knew he should hate them. He did, in fact hate them. But they were still Fictional Personae. And like any true soldier who had seen the face of worthy adversary, he respected them as well. "Not like this," he whispered to himself. "Please, not like this."

Enraged, Mama Bear threw herself at the back door, overlooking the vicious furrows her claws tore in the back of her husband's hide in her rage. She became stuck in the frame, sandwiched between the bulk of her husband below her and the unyielding door jam above. Without leverage to pull free and too blinded by fury to pull back, she was all but helpless against Goldie.

The soldier closed his eyes and wished he could close his ears as well. But there was no escaping the demons in his head, dancing in the darkness behind his eyelids to the symphony of dull thuds of heavy pipe against meat, muscle, and bone, and the keening wail of the bear child. He fumbled within his jacket, seeking his last remaining memento from his old days of soldiering. His fingers closed over the hilt like a prayer, and it felt comforting in his grip. He held it to him like faith, and eventually the sounds of growling stopped. But still the merciless beating continued for several minutes.

The bear child growled through the tears. "I should kill you."

The soldier did not open his eyes, his head and hand still tightly wrapped around his own violent past. He could think of no argument to dissuade her otherwise. "Maybe. Maybe you should. I led her here, after all."

The little bear stood and approached him. He could feel her claws upon his stubbled cheek. "We wanted someone to lead her to us. It is why papa left you alive in the gutter after killing the little one. Golden hair took everything. Mama and Papa..." she choked on the words, and even with his eyes closed, he could tell she was crying softly. "Mama and Papa just wanted to take something of hers. She came into our house. She is the one who broke the laws, she is the bad one. Not us. We were the victim and she is the hero. Where is the justice in that?"

The soldier realized that the claws were gone. He opened his eyes and looked into the tear-red eyes of a little girl. A Fictional Personae, like him, she was more alone in the world than before. A creak on the floorboards behind the little bear girl drew both their attention.

With the back door now blocked, Goldie must have let herself in through an upstairs window. It had taken a little while for her to make her way to the kitchen. She stood in the doorway, only a few feet away. Her heavy pipe was matted with blood and fur, bobbing eagerly in her grip. "I'm the hero. You're just an animal."

The little bear didn't even flinch when Goldie crushed her skull. But her eyes said everything, right up until the second they went blank and lifeless. The soldier watched the little body fall to the ground, turning into a bear even as she fell. "This wasn't a good world for you anyway," he whispered to the corpse. "You wouldn't have liked it here."

Goldie moved to the steadfast soldier, and helped him to his feet. Her smile was broad—proud and satisfied. To the soldier's mind, that smile was unjustified. "We won," she said without surprise, as if the ending had been pre-ordained.

The soldier shook his head, holding onto Goldie's shoulder with one hand for support, the other still deep within his jacket, wrapped around the hilt of his bayonet. "No. No one won today."

Her expression showed she didn't understand. The soldier suspected that she never would. He pulled the old army bayonet out of his jacket, his knuckles white around the worn grip. He considered plunging it into Goldie and killing her, just to bring the circle to a close.

But there had been too much ink spilled today already. Instead, he let her see it before he tossed it to the floor.

The young killer had already lost interest in the steadfast soldier. She turned her attention to wiping her pipe clean on a kitchen towel. He resolved to hobble away quickly, before people showed up asking too many questions. So many bodies, Fictional or otherwise, was bound to raise some eyebrows. He spared one last look down at little bear before he left. "There are no happy endings. Not here." The soldier left through the front door, vanishing quickly in the thick Chelsea fog like a drop of ink in water.

♦

Nathan Crowder is an award-winning writer of fiction with southwest roots, currently living in the rainy Pacific Northwest. A certified coffee and micro-brew aficionado, he is a gregarious and happy guy who can see the silver lining in any cloud, though this is rarely reflected in his writing. His fiction has ranged across many genres, but he is generally happiest in the urban fantasy, horror, mystery, or super-hero arena. A life-long geek for social justice, history, sociology, architecture, film, and music, Nathan has a special interest in how public and shared art reflects culture and community. He is the proud author of the Cobalt Universe super-hero adventure novels, including *Greetings from Buena Rosa, Ride Like the Devil, Cobalt City Blues,* and *Chanson Noir.*

nathancrowder.com

"The Prey"

by Bruce Taylor

"'nother beer," the Something whispered, "have another beer."

Mack sat in the Blue Light Bar and Grill and the memory appeared of Lucy, her hair long and blonde, beneath him, moving with him, and he felt the deliciousness of her body, her excitement and he said, "Oh, God, Lucy, oh, God, God, I'm coming—"

"Jesus," she said, "oh, just like that, just like that—oh, oh, God—"

They orgasmically exploded within seconds of the other. Then, lying in each others arms, their hearts pounding, they cuddled, kissed, and he said, "God, that was wonderful. I never want to leave you."

Lucy had that warm, infectious laugh and said, "Don't you dare, lover. Don't you *dare*."

(The Something knew differently, but at that time it was quiet. It didn't have to say anything. Just being there was enough.)

And it was good. So good. The laughter, the loving. They were young, and life looked so long and so lovely ahead of them. The family picnics, the shared holidays. The joy of companionship and love. He would never dream of leaving her.

Even when Mack embezzled from the firm—

♦ "Another beer," and the Something made a sound like weeping.

Still, Mack thought the good times would never end. And during the time in jail, he had time to think about it. To think that it would be okay. It would still be okay, after all.

Hendricks, vice president of the firm, a portly guy with black hair seemingly always plastered at an angle to his forehead, and with a gold front tooth, came to visit Mack frequently at first.

"Lots of people do it," said Mack. "What I did wasn't all that bad. The Government cheats people all the time."

Hendricks tried. God knows he tried. "What can I tell you?" he sighed. "We've been through this before. Calvin—Calvin Smyth—one of the most respected CEOs in the city—the guy who sought you out for regional manager because of your excellent work— don't you think he was disappointed by what you did? After that big salary boost to boot? You were already making good money, man, why'd you do it? Why'd you do it? You fucked up your family, your reputation—"

And Mack remembered waving his hand. "Ah, come on, after I'm out everyone will forget. It's like it will never have happened."

He said it in a voice that certainly sounded like his own, but somehow, someway, it seemed like Something Else was talking.

Hendricks sat, mouth open in disbelief. Finally he said, "Don't you have any conscience? Don't you fucking care that you hurt people? That you disappointed them? Much less destroyed your credibility? Don't you care?"

"Hey," Mack laughed with a laugh that was his, but kind of not his, like Something Else was laughing, "I made a mistake, okay? It won't happen again. Never again."

Hendricks just looked at Mack through the plexiglass at the jail's visiting area. "I want to believe you, but I don't."

He didn't come back for a while. A long while. A lot of people stopped coming by and soon, aside from his jail pals, with whom he got along very well, Mack was quite alone—except for that Something that began to grow even stronger in him.

"You could really use a drink," it said. It scampered about a bit more in Mack these days. Especially at night, when he slept, and his father stomped through his heart, cursing, yelling, "Fucking banks don't know what they're fucking talking about. Closed my account again! There was plenty of money in there two weeks ago! What do they know?" and *crash,* his bottle went flying against the fireplace hearth as it did so many times and the sweet-sour smell of whisky permeated the air, a sour perfume and the glass showered over the wall, the rug, over Mack—a child, cowering against the chair.

Mack dared to look at his father and saw him somehow with the face of a spider, the black eyes, his arms waving about like an insect waving its legs, that mindless insect hate, and Mack hated him and feared him but strangely, strangely loved him, especially when his father saw Mack cowering there, and then he'd look for a long, long time and finally would stumble over to Mack, pull him up, clumsily hold him and then sobbing, say, "I made a mistake. It'll never happen again. Oh, God, Mackie, I'm sorry I did it again, Sonny Boy. Oh, *God,* could I use a drink!"

The fact that the Something sounded like his father's voice eluded Mack. He would then close his eyes and, thinking about the embezzlement, would say to himself,

"It'll be ok. It'll be ok. I just made a mistake. It'll never happen again. Everybody makes mistakes." What was particularly soothing was that many of his jail pals said the same thing. He must be on the right track.

♦ "A drink would be good right now," Something said when they let Mack out of jail. He felt it scramble and move within him, and it give him a mind-picture of a drink in his hand, feeling comfortable, at peace, like it was all ok now. All done, forgotten. Time to get a job, leave the past behind, get on with life again. People are forgiving. People forget. Many had done worse than what he had done and had gone on to live perfectly fine and respectable lives. What he had done wasn't *really* all *that* bad, and so forth and so on, and it was time to get on with life.

Hendricks at the firm was not in. No one knew when he would return. "Yes, we'll take your number. Yes, yes, Mack Giles. Of *course*, we remember you. We have another call, goodbye."

"Yes, this is Lucy. Mack? You son of a bitch. How'd you get my number? How *dare* you call me! You lying, fucking, cheating—don't *ever* call me again!" *Slam!*

Mack heard that Something think, what's wrong with her?

"This is Hermanita Reboza—Mack? Mack! Honey, when you get outta jail, huh?"

"Well, just today and, uh, it's like this, I could really use a—"

"No, no, honey, no more favors—you run off an' you lef' me an' tha's not okay. You really 'urt me an' I like you an' all that but I no let you 'urt me like tha' again. No, no, I cry lotsa tears for you an' you no answer my phone calls an' letters—no, no."

"Hey, I'm sorry, I was under a lot of stress, I mean, the bum rap with the firm, and I didn't deserve that. I'm a good guy, you know I didn't mean to…."

"No, no, Mack, you say tha' before too an' I believe you but I no believe you now—your words and your actions like night and day an' I always say that actions they talk better'n words so you go 'way. Bye." *Click.*

"Jesus," said Mack to that Something, "Jesus. Would you listen to that. After all I did for her. Wow."

"God, you really need a drink now," Something responded. First priority. He felt Something in him move his feet, steer his body, focus his eyes on the sign nearby: Blue Light Bar and Grill.

Dazed, he walked and for whatever reason, a scene jumped into his head; his mother in the car, driving off, suitcases piled in the back, leaving Mack with his father, and his father throwing a beer bottle after the car and yelling, "Fucking bitch! Why you leaving me? What'd I do? God, the least you coulda done was take Mack! I don't know how to take care of no kid!"

Something icy stabbed Mack in the heart. Or was it something stabbing from the inside—out? Mack's thoughts became like useless babble; the past taking over the present, the present lost to the past in a swirling, black snow/slow vortex and in the middle of it, the form, the legs, the intense eyes, black as his father's.

"I need a drink to calm my nerves," his father always said.

Mack remembered thinking that he must have had a *lot* of nerves that needed steadying. But his father always looked better after he drank, and when he fell asleep and passed out, he was just fine. Peaceful. Calm. Mack liked that.

The Blue Light Bar and Grill had a happy hour. Mack was there at the right time. The right evening. The right night, until he was hoisted out of the seat and pushed out the door at three a.m. He staggered, found an alleyway and collapsed against a wall. Something struggled and fought within him. Another stabbing pain, and another, colder pain in his chest and as Mack sat there, he had the dim impression of something escaping from him, wrapping him in some sort of silky, sticky substance, and then dragging him away; he looked up to see that he was being pulled by a dark, bulbous thing and his last thought, as he closed his eyes was, "Boy, I could *really* use a drink!"

And vaguely, he heard an icy whispering, "You can say that again, Sonny Boy."

♦

Bruce Taylor, aka "Mr Magic Realism," writes magic realism and bizarre literature. His book, *Kafka's Uncle and Other Strange Stories* was nominated for the &NOW Award for Innovative Writing. Eraserhead Press published his book: *Mr. Magic Realism,* and he co-authored *Stormworld* with Brian Herbert.

The second book of his spiritual trilogy, *Magic of Wild Places,* is under editorial consideration. The first book, *Mountains of the Night* was released by The Landis Review.

Bruce is also a hypnotherapist and makes time in all of this to sit with Purrrzac, his cat, and admire the smashing view of Mt. Rainier from his writing loft.

BruceBTaylor.com

"Honoring the Dead"

by Jennifer Brozek

♦ Battle

The battle was a slaughter and it was meant to be one. Guard Captain Waithe knew this was true the moment the kill order came in. What should have been a simple exercise in quelling a riot became an example and a message to the Purist Believers everywhere. When the military and the police were rolled into one, all a commanding guardsman could do was obey and try to do his best for both his guardsmen and the people he was protecting. He also tried to do his worst to those he fought against.

Sometimes, those people were one and the same.

Like now.

The guardsmen squad had set up behind protected barriers in front of the walled hospital where the only living survivor of this latest round of Believer attacks against the Hedari explorers lay helpless within; his life hanging by a thread. A thread these Believers wanted to snap. *'Not that I blame them,'* he thought. Then the Guard Captain put his own personal feelings aside and looked to his men.

The squad's orders were to put down any attacks against the hospital and bring the leaders of the local cult on this planet to justice. This newest round of attacks had started just over an hour ago. First it was only a march that became a stand-off that morphed into the series of rioting charges that battered at the riot barrier the guardsmen had erected. Each one of these charges had been quelled with firepower and the resulting bodies still lay in the street.

"Why do they keep coming?" Guardsman Kintares asked, his voice breaking with held back tears as he kept his weapon pointed at the chaos of rioters preparing to attack again. "They don't have real weapons. They can't win."

"Stand your ground, Guardsman. Do your duty." It was the only safe answer the Guard Captain could give from his elevated vantage point behind his squad. If he tried to give a real answer, his men would see them as people again and not the enemy. His men would die and he could not, would not, have that. He stood there, surveying the battlefield with only part of his mind. The other part of it answered his guardsman's question.

They come, he thought, *because it's all they know to do. They come because they have a* Cause *they won't turn from and that* Cause *is treason against the empire. For that reason alone, we kill them.* If he could have, he would have wiped the sweat from his head. But, to remove your helmet on the battlefield was to invite death in.

Then all time for introspection was done and his earpiece came to life, "We've got another charge and it's huge - funneling in from the three side streets. Biggest one yet, Guard Captain. Out." The guardsman on the other end of the communication sounded amazed and terrified.

"Received. Out." As Waithe responded, he was already turning to shout orders to his men. They were the same orders he had been shouting off and on for the last hour. "Here they come! Termination ordered! Shoot to kill! Shoot to kill!" He paused and added, "Don't let them cross my line, guardsmen! Not a single one!"

This time, the fighting was fiercer. Though the rioters were not armed with the same high tech, heavy armament that the guardsmen had, they did have weapons—low tech, but still deadly—and they had the numbers. A squad of thirty men had been put down to quell the riot of 'three hundred' and bring the cult leaders in for the murder of two Hedari explorers as well as for the attempted murder of the third. Only that 'three hundred' had been closer to three thousand. The bloodshed was horrific especially since they were fighting civilians and not professional soldiers.

As all thirty of his men alternated firing and ducking for cover, Waithe patrolled their backside, shoring up their defenses in the line. He had the overview lay of the land and this was the dirtiest kind of fighting—in the middle of a city. The collateral damage was overwhelming. Only the walled and protected hospital building behind him was still standing and some of its walls would need to be rebuilt. He shot two rioters breaking through on the right flank and saw one of his men had fallen.

Jumping down from his higher vantage point, he shouted, "Man down! Right flank, close that hole! Close it!" while he ran to Guardsman Ermath's side. He pulled the man back behind the line of fire and checked for a pulse. The guardsman was already dead. Waithe gave a curse and took the man's ID chit, stuffing it into his pocket. Then, time for the dead was done.

He got back up to his outlook post and shot three more rioters as they converged on the line. That, along with the firepower of his center men, drove back the forward middle portion of the charge, breaking it apart. After that, the organized charge became an incoherent riot again. Thirty seconds later, it was a rout. Those who were not running away stayed where they were because they would never move, or care about anything else, ever again.

From his vantage point, he saw that a man on the left flank was down. It was Guardsman Spiradon and there was a lot of blood around him. Guardsman Kintares was crouched over him, his hands bloody from trying to keep his friend and squadmate alive. He had his back to the line and while that should have been the death of him with a shot to the back, it was not. Death took a different form.

"Damnit," Waithe muttered. He took one last look and started back down from the high ground towards his downed men. In the seconds it took him to look down, set his feet on the rubble and look up again, death had reappeared.

After the last of the weapons fire ended and silence descended, death came for Guardsman Kintares in the form of a teenaged girl. She came out of one of the broken side buildings on the left and sprinted towards him with a homemade bomb in her hands. Kintares turned his head and froze, just staring at the girl as she ran silently towards him with murder in her eyes. By the time Guard Captain Waithe and Guardsman Tascen opened fire on her, she was on top of Kintares and Spiradon. She set off the bomb as she was hit from two directions.

Kintares never shifted from his frozen, crouched position over Spiradon's body. He did not make a single move for his weapon. He just watched her come. One moment he was crouched down, the next moment he, Spiradon, and the girl were blown to pieces with body parts flying in all directions. Coda, Dram and Thymi, the three closest guardsmen to the left flank, were also hit in the explosion but only the girl, Kintares and Spiradon were killed. It was the last attack of a suicidal cultist and it was the most painful by far.

◆ Aftermath

Guard Captain Waithe sat at his desk in his office in the Guard Headquarters building on the prime planet. The office was clean enough to pass inspection and decorated in a manner as to be unmistakably 'career military.' Plaques and commendations lined the wall in orderly rows. The desk was clear of all debris. A neat pile of paperwork demanding his attention sat at his left hand and the only adornment that showed that the office was inhabited by a man was the picture of a pretty dark haired woman placed upon the desk that could have been a wife, a girlfriend or a sister.

He stared at his computer screen for a long time without moving. This was the part of his job, his duty to the empire, that he hated most. There were three names on his screen with their locations of the next of kin. Two had parents. One had a wife. The parents, he knew from experience, would be the easier visits to make. Parents had a way of accepting that their child was going into danger when they joined the Guard. Wives did not. Not usually.

However, this was not a task he would shove off on one of his many assistant junior guardsmen. Although they were all military men and women themselves, Waithe did not believe they would give the dead their due. They would not understand the gravity of the situation until they led men and women into battle themselves and watched some of them die at their command. No, *Announcements of the Honored Dead* should have the attention of someone who truly understood.

Thus, it was his job and his duty; a heavy one, but one that these guardsmen all deserved.

He touched the first name on the screen in his list. Guardsman Ermath. The official form of *Death in Battle* opened up and he began to type. It was all standard stuff until it came to the last part where he was to put his official personal condolences that would be placed under the official *Announcement* document. Both of these documents would be delivered to the next of kin with the guardsman's personal effects. He hesitated, thinking of the right words to say because, unlike other Guard Captains, he would be delivering the news personally.

Finally, he wrote.

My deepest sympathies for your loss. Guardsman Ermath was an excellent guardsman and one who always thought of his peers first. I cannot think of a day that he did not look to his friends and family within the Guard to see what hurts he could soothe. Always one with a kind word, Guardsman Ermath will be sorely missed. He died doing his duty and it was a good death. Our objective was achieved. He did not die in vain. Be proud of Guardsman Ermath. I am and I honor his memory. ~ Guard Captain Waithe

He worked on Guardsman Spiradon's *Announcement* next and wrote a similar heartfelt message of condolence tailored to the guardsman's taciturn ways but willingness to teach those who wished to learn. Waithe felt that sense of loss again as he finished up the official documentation and his computer screen focused on the last guardsman *Announcement* document to be completed. Guardsman Kintares.

Waithe opened the document with a touch of his finger and all but rushed through the form, because he had written this part twice before. Then he got to the personal condolences section. When he reached this point, he sat back and considered what to say. *Kintares had been a good guardsman. Not the best and not the worst,* he thought. *He was...had been...in the middle of the pack and destined never to command his own squad. That didn't make him a bad man.*

However, Waithe could not get the image of a frozen Kintares, crouched over Spiradon's body, watching the suicidal girl come, out of his mind. He could not stop himself from wincing again and again as he, himself, was too late to stop her and the bomb went off, killing his men. The Guard Captain could not stop seeing the blood and guts on the ground behind the stop line or his men's severed limbs twitching in the dirt. He had seen bodies before. Yes. But these were his people. His guardsmen. His. When the bodies were his people, it was never easy to dismiss them.

Do I blame him for his lack? Waithe wondered. He turned to the computer, pulled up the footage from the battle and replayed this particular incident again. It was a deliberate thing as seen through the unfeeling eye of the camera instead of through the filter of painful flashes of memory. The camera had been mounted high on the hospital wall to cover all of the grounds right outside of the hospital entrance where the guardsmen had set their line. Waithe watched the fighting as the video timer counted the seconds and minutes.

He paused the footage the instant before the shots hit the girl and the bomb exploded. He studied the scene and tried to see it as Kintares must have seen it. Then, a small detail came into focus. Waithe restarted the footage and let it play through. He replayed the scene two more times before shifting his focus from the moments of Guardsman Kitares' death to earlier in the battle. Specifically, to the point at which Guardsman Spiradon fell.

Low tech though the Believers were, that did not make their weapons any less deadly than the high tech firepower of the guardsmen. Men have been killing each other with swords for thousands of years. While it seems crazy that a sword could kill an elite guardsman in this day and age, just because a civilization advances does not mean a sword is any less deadly. It was a sword that had taken down Spiradon. A lucky strike through the chest by a young man with only one arm. The other arm had been shot off just above the elbow.

Waithe watched as Spiradon fell, Kintares killed the sword wielder, checked the area for enemies and then turned to Spiradon's supine body. Kintares' next action made up Waithe's mind for him. He returned to his document and began to write his final thoughts on Guardsman Kintares.

♦ Offer

Waithe sat in his office, ruminating over the choice to make Guardsman Kintares a hero instead of a failure when, in fact, the man had been both in one. He had worked to save his squadmate from a lethal wound but he had frozen when he should have acted. What Waithe could not decide now was whether or not Kintares had frozen because the attacker had been a teenage girl or because he knew if he removed his hands from Spiradon's chest, the Spiradon would die.

It's all speculation and hindsight at this point, he thought with a scowl. *Both men are dead and the proper forms had been fulfilled. Let it go.*

The suddenly tossed coin did not startle Waithe. Instead, it was a welcome distraction. He caught it with the automatic reflexes of a trained guardsman and looked up. "Hedari Araquez. What's this for?"

"Your thoughts." The handsome young man smiled briefly as he walked into the room and closed the door.

"You don't want them." Waithe eyed his visitor, taking in the information his senses could glean. Full Explorer uniform, a serious attitude and the closed office door. "And you aren't here for a social visit. Otherwise, we would have had this talk in my quarters."

"Sometimes, I think you live here." Araquez took a seat across from Waithe with the ease of long time familiarity.

"Be that as it may, what can I do for you?"

"First, you may congratulate me on my new position. Mission Commander Hedari Araquez at your service." Araquez gave a little bow from his seat.

Waithe eyed the man. Araquez had meant the gesture to be light and casual. Instead, it had revealed just how uncertain he was. *Why would you be uncertain about me of all people?* Waithe wondered as he said, "Congratulations. What's the mission?"

"That's what I'm here to speak to you about. A star system has been found with at least one habitable planet. The new Explorer class ship will be going. Compliment of five thousand. I need a Guard Commander for the mission."

Waithe sat back and considered his friend's words. A new, viable system was a rare and precious thing. "I'm a Guard Captain." He gestured to his rank pin.

"That will change."

"Why me?"

"Because you're the best, in my opinion." Araquez paused at the look that Waithe gave him. "Because we need to go to this planet. The Empress' oracles say that a great danger lies there but the Empire's only salvation is there as well. It's dangerous and I need to know that the person who's going to be leading the Guard is someone I can trust."

Waithe nodded. "What's the catch?"

That startled a laugh out of Araquez. "I tell you that we are going into certain danger and you want to know what the catch is?"

Waithe was not smiling. "Yes. Tell me what you are not saying. The thing that makes you believe I'll tell you 'No.' despite your offer of a promotion, exploration and certain danger."

Araquez looked away and then looked back again, looking Waithe straight in the eyes. "Based on the nature of the danger, the crew complement will be about ten percent Hedari." When Waithe gave no immediate response, he continued. "I know you don't like our kind. I know I'm one of the few you tolerate. But we need you. I know you'll protect the Hedari— most of them scientists—despite your personal feelings."

Waithe reached out towards the picture of the dark haired woman but did not pick it up. "I lost my sister to you people. She died because she became Hedari. Now, you're asking me to protect five hundred of you?" His tone was soft and deliberate.

"Yes." Araquez nodded.

"Why?"

"Because, I know you. I know you're a good Captain and will be a great Commander. I trust you with your people, the Explorers Guild's people...and with my people. There are few that I can say that about. We need you. The Empress will approve your promotion and your new assignment if I can assure her that you'll accept it."

Waithe frowned. "The Empress is involved personally?"

Araquez nodded again.

He returned the nod. "I'll think about it. I'll give you my decision as soon as I can."

It was a dismissive statement and Araquez understood it to be so. He stood, bowed and left without another word. Waithe watched him go, knowing already what his answer would be. But he needed time to think about the ramifications of that answer.

Also, he had another, more important, job to do first.

♦ Announcement

He arrived at Guardsman Kintares' home last. Partly because he wanted to save the hardest for last, and partly, because the guardsman's home planet was the farthest one out from the Headquarters planet. Planet Ixon was in the Hayes system and was one of the two main water supply planets for this end of the system. A lot of family men were stationed here out of deference to their families and were called away for a tour of duty several times a year to the more dangerous sectors of space.

While he was home, Guardsman Kintares had been an Acquisitions man for Base Aramanthe, making sure that all the equipment needed by the base was there. Not an exciting job but an important one nonetheless.

By all accounts, he did his job well and he would be missed.

One of the junior guardsmen gave Waithe a ride to Guardsman Kintares' home. While on the way, he reviewed Guardsman Kintares' culture and how to appropriately address his widow. In this case, it was a first name situation. *'Gennabelle, his wife and Natara, his daughter,'* he thought, mentally repeating the names with the correct pronunciation. He knew these coming few moments would impact Gennabelle and Natara for the rest of their lives and he wanted to make sure these memories would be as good as they could be under the circumstances.

"Please stay here. I won't be long." Waithe told his impromptu chauffeur.

"Yes, Guard Captain." The guardsman sat back and prepared to wait for as long as necessary.

Guard Captain Waithe stood and pulled his Class A uniform in line. Even though he was a small, stocky man, he knew he was an impressive figure in this uniform designed more for the grips and grins of social events with aristocrats and leaders than for the somber occasion he was about to undertake. Still, the widow Kintares deserved the news delivered by someone who cared and looked like it.

He knocked on her door and waited. When Gennabella opened the door, he waited and watched her very carefully. She had a smile on her face when the door opened. He watched as her eyes flicked over him, taking in the information presented. First to his face, then to his rank, then his medals and finally his name. He saw the recognition wake in her eyes as she recognized the name. Her smile faltered as the realization of what a visit from her husband's Tour of

Duty commanding officer might mean. Then, he watched her face go neutral, all emotions hidden.

"Hello Guard Captain. What may I do for you?"

"Hello Gennabelle. I have news. May I come in?" His voice was soft and courteous.

She nodded and stepped aside, closing the door after him. She said nothing as she passed him in the hall and led him to the main room of the living quarters. As he stepped in, she asked, "May I get you something to drink?"

"No. I thank you."

"It is nothing."

"It is to me." He said, completing the standard gratitude ritual. He paused for a beat before he asked, "Is Natara home? She may wish to be here for this."

"I'm here." The voice came from behind them. Natara stepped forward. Her face was also a mask of neutrality.

The moment that Waithe saw Natara, he was glad of what he had decided to do for his dead guardsman.

Both mother and daughter sat on the couch across from the chair Waithe chosen. He placed the box of personal effects next to him, opened his case and chose not to notice the collective wince at the sight of the *Announcement for the Honored Dead* certificate. He picked it up and handed it over to Gennabella. "My deepest condolences," he said as she took the document from him.

"What happened?" Natara asked, looking up from the paper. "How did my father die?"

Guard Captain Waithe did not say, "Well, Natara, he froze in the middle of battle because a girl who could have been your twin ran at him with a homemade bomb. He saw you in her and died because of it."

What Guard Captain Waithe said instead was, "He died on the line while trying to save the life of one of his squadmates. He had his hands full, covering a sucking chest wound when a suicide bomber came in and killed all three of them. Your father died a hero and he is to be honored as such. He will receive a metal for his bravery under fire."

"I...we appreciate this." Gennabelle said. Her voice was soft and controlled. "More than you know."

"I have Guardsman Kintares' things with me." He indicated the box at his side. He watched the pair of them and understood the reaction to the news of death affected each differently. In this family, the chain of command, and the decorum that went with it, held tight.

Gennabelle stood. "If you don't mind, Guard Captain, I will open that in private."

He stood and handed the box to Gennabelle. He watched her walk out, leaving him alone with Natara. He turned his attention to the teenager and saw that while her face was still neutral, her eyes had a suspiciously wet and shiny look to them. "Tears are nothing to be ashamed of, Natara," he said, wanting to soothe her in some small way.

"A Guardsman's daughter doesn't cry. My father taught me this." Her voice was tight with control and brittle with pain.

Waithe nodded at her. He did not push. This family would mourn in private. Tears would not be shared with a commanding officer. In this family, that was inappropriate.

"Did he really die a good death?" She looked him in the face, judging him, watching him for signs of falsehood.

He could see this was a very important question to her and nodded his affirmation. "He did. He died a hero."

"I'm going to be just as good and as brave as he was. I'm going to be a Guardsman as soon as I'm of age."

There was a desperation in the declaration that Waithe understood far too well. Part of him wanted to encourage her path. Part of him wanted to dissuade her. *'You're too young to be thinking of military service. You should be out there dating boys and wondering what to wear,'* He thought. But, as he knew, children of a Guardsman grew up living a very different life than other children. In the end, he simply asked, "Do you say so?"

She nodded at him.

"Then may it be so."

Those were the last words he spoke to her. As soon as Gennabelle returned, he took his leave. She paused at the front door. "Thank you for your words of condolence. They mean a lot. Natara will appreciate them, too."

At that point, he could not say "It is nothing." To him, it was something. He elected, instead, to say, "I meant those words." He nodded to her and returned to the waiting guardsman and his transport without looking back. After all, Guard Captain Waithe, who would soon to be Guard Commander Waithe, had a new assignment to go to.

The question of whether or not to serve on the new Hedari explorer ship was never really a question at all. His duty was to the empire and to her needs no matter how hard the job would be. He had just lost three good men in the defense of a single Hedari explorer. He had known then that going in to quell the riot that such a possibility existed and did not hesitate then.

He would not hesitate now.

This time, though, with a complement of five thousand, fifteen hundred would be guardsmen to protect, manage and serve the three thousand explorers and five hundred Hedari. Tours of duty on an explorer ship were never easy. Too much could go wrong. This tour of duty would not have an end date because a new system was involved.

But 'easy' was not what he expected when he signed up to serve. It never had been and it never would be. He nodded to himself, pulled out his hand-held and looked at his waiting communications. Araquez sent over the details of what the tour of duty would entail the same day they met. Waithe finally opened the communiqué and began to read. The Empire needed him and it was his duty to serve.

♦

Jennifer Brozek is a freelance author for many RPG companies including Margaret Weis Productions, Savage Mojo, Rogue Games, and Catalyst Game Labs. Winner of the *2010 Origins Award for Best Roleplaying Game Supplement*, her contributions to RPG sourcebooks include *Dragonlance, Colonial Gothic, Shadowrun, Serenity, Savage Worlds,* and White Wolf SAS.

Winner of the *2009 Australian Shadows Award* for edited publication, Jennifer has edited 3 anthologies with more on the way. Author of *In a Gilded Light* and *The Little Finance Book That Could*, she has more than 25 published short stories, is the creator and editor of the semiprozine, *The Edge of Propinquity*, and is an editor for the Apex Book Company.

She also writes the monthly gaming column *Dice & Deadlines*. When she is not writing her heart out, she is gallivanting around the Pacific Northwest in its wonderfully mercurial weather. Jennifer is a member of Broad Universe, SFWA and HWA.

jennifer-brozek.livejournal.com

Jennifer Brozek

"Small Cold Things"

by Richard E. Dansky

It hit Jenny when she woke up: the smell.

"Not again," she whispered. "Oh, God, please not again." Faintly, she could hear rushing water. The shower was running, the bathroom door closed—maybe there was enough time to hide it before Sean came back out. Questing fingers trawled across the bed sheets while she forced her eyes to crack open, looking for the evidence she already knew would be there.

In the bed.

Again.

Fingertips found what they were looking for, a damp patch still faintly warm to the touch. No wonder the scent had awakened her. It hung in the air, acrid and dense. Two senses were in agreement that it was there; she screwed her eyes back shut in hopes of providing the third, but still brought her wet fingertips to her nose for conformation.

God no God no oh God no.

Jenny sniffed.

The stink flooded its way up her sinuses, rattled around inside her head, and forced her eyelids open from the inside. With a gasp, Jenny sat up, holding the tainted hand away from herself as if it had been dipped in poison. There was no mistaking what she had found on the traitor fingertips, none at all.

Cat pee.

In the bed.

Again.

"Mwraor?" A furry head poked its way over the edge of the bed, disappeared for a moment, and then re-emerged attached to a scandalously plump Siamese. "Mwraor?" the cat said again, and snuggled up to her, purring.

"Bad Lucy. Bad cat," she said, but there was no heat in it. There never was.

Lucy looked up at her and purred, and with a sigh Jenny resigned herself to the inevitable. She reached down and gave the cat a quick scratch behind the ears with her clean hand, and Lucy leaned up and into it.

"That only encourages her, you know."

Jenny looked up. Sean had come out of the bathroom dripping wet, a towel around his waist, his expression one of weary disgust. "You could at least say 'bad kitty' or something."

"I don't think she understands English." Jenny's reply was skittish, defensive. She swung her legs over the side of the bed, gingerly probing the carpet with her toes for anything that might have seen the inside of one of the cats. Finding nothing, she hoisted herself up and started pulling the sheets off the bed. Sean, arms folded across his chest, just watched her. "Again?" he asked.

She nodded, head down, not trusting herself to look at him. "Again. I'll take care of it. It's my turn."

"Yes," he said. "It is," and turned back into the bathroom. "I need to get ready for work. So do you. Don't spend too long on the damn cats, okay?"

He didn't wait for an answer before heading back into the bathroom; he knew there wouldn't be one. The door shut resoundingly behind him as Jenny screwed her eyes shut and punched the tainted sheets into a ball. Jumping down from the bed, Lucy preened and rubbed her legs, but Jenny ignored her. Both cats—Lucy and her playmate Sally—had the best and most scientifically appropriate of everything. Special food to prevent UTIs, special noisemakers and pads to keep them away from certain parts of the house, special this and that and the other thing, all purchased with the sole intent of making sure they didn't use the entire house as one giant, carpeted litter box.

To date, none of it had worked for more than 72 hours at a stretch. The bills had racked up and so had the hours spent scrubbing cat piss out of carpets and cat vomit off the walls, all to no avail. And each incident ratcheted up the tension a little higher, added another coal under the steady, simmering conflict between her and Sean.

It was the only thing she and Sean fought over, but with all its permutations, they didn't need anything else. He'd walk in the door and make a complaint about the stink, or one of the cats would throw up on the bed, and they'd be at it again. It wasn't violent, just constant. Somehow the cats had become the only thing in their lives, and she could feel it strangling everything else they had.

The sound of scratching distracted her. She looked over, and there was Sally, whaling away at the bathroom door with her front paws like a feline John Henry. "Oh, no," she breathed, dropping the sheets and darting over to pull the black-and-white mutt kitty away from the door. She caught Sally in her arms and pulled her away, even as the door cracked open. "Honey?" Sean began, even as Sally let out an ear-splitting yowl and twisted, paws flailing. A couple of claws caught Jenny across the meat of her left hand, dragging across and digging deep.

"Sally!" Sean shouted, as Jenny dropped her and blood filled the scratched furrows. "Bad girl!" He took a few quick steps forward, even as the cat scrambled out of the room. Lucy backed under the bed and hissed.

"Jesus, sweetie, are you all right?" Sean turned to her, eyes full of concern. "You're bleeding."

Jenny brushed the blood away with her thumb, shaking her head. "Don't worry about it. It's nothing. I don't want you to get blood on your shirt."

"Screw that," he said, and strode off to get a handful of tissues. "Direct pressure," he said when he returned, "and there's Neosporin in the-"

"I know, I know." She waved him off. "You need to get to work, Sean, and I'm a big girl. Don't worry."

"Are you sure?" he said, but his feet were already taking him toward the door.

"I'm sure," she said, and dabbed at the blood with the tissues. It came up in spots and lines. A faint "I love you," drifted up from downstairs, punctuated by doors opening and closing.

"I love you, too," Jenny whispered. "Have a nice day." She waited for the sound of his car to fade away before she let herself move toward the bathroom, and the shower, and the start of her day. The last sound she heard before she shut the door was Lucy, yowling mournfully as she began to claw at the furniture.

♦ Sean's car was in the garage when Jenny got home.

That was unusual; most nights, he worked an hour or two later than she did. She parked and sat for a minute, trying to find the nerve to get out of the car. Getting out of the car meant finding out why he was home so early. She imagined the scene in her head, imagined it ending badly twenty different ways.

It'll be fine, she told herself, hand frozen on the ignition. *He's just home early. It's nothing to worry about. Just go inside and talk to him.* And then, a minute later, *When this song is over.*

It was three songs and the end of the CD before Jenny finally killed the engine, and another minute after that before she let herself out. She stared at the door for a minute, then looked away.

Her eye caught something: a wet sycamore leaf plastered to the hood of Sean's Acura, dark against the white paint. *I'll just take that off for him before I go in,* she thought. *He hates that sort of mess. It'll make him happy if I pull the leaf off.*

She walked over to his car. *I'll just grab the leaf and then we'll go in. That's all.*

The garage door grumbled shut behind her as she tentatively reached out to pluck the offending leaf. Her fingertips brushed the surface of the hood as she did so.

It was cool. He'd been home for a while, then, alone in the house with the cats. For no reason that she could fathom, that particular thought worried her. The leaf fell, forgotten, as she hurried to the door.

The mud room was dark as she turned the key, as was the hallway beyond it. Even the kitchen light, normally as constant as the sunrise, was off. "Honey," she called. "Are you OK?" The smell hit her like a hammer when she walked in the door, sharp and pungent. It was like this every day, but after a couple of breaths, as always, she found she could ignore it. Not Sean, though. He was a little more sensitive about it. It was hard for him.

"I'm fine," his words drifted back. "I'm just thinking."

"Is everything all right?" She drifted through the kitchen and into the den, barely spotting the silhouette of his head against the gloom. He was seated on the couch, lights out and television off, and a low purring told her that one of the cats was probably curled up in his lap.

"Everything's fine." His voice was low and even. He never got loud when he got angry; that was one of the things she loved about him. He never shouted. He just explained, relentlessly, how he was right and she was wrong and how it would be best if she just let him take care of whatever needed doing.

Most of the time, she simply did. The rest, she argued for a few minutes until he talked her into letting him have his way anyway. Now, though, she suddenly wished he would simply act, just go ahead and do something instead of wearing her down with words.

But he wouldn't do that. He'd never do that. Instead, he turned and looked back at her over his shoulder. His voice was as soft and measured as ever, and he said, "We need to talk."

He's leaving. That was her first thought. He'd finally had enough and he was leaving. Hesitantly, she took the three steps that led her into the den.

"What's wrong?" she asked, and hated herself for the quaver in her voice. *He's not leaving. He can't be.* She stared at him, silently pleading with him to at least look at her, to face her when he dropped the bombshell.

His eyes strayed back to the floor.

"Look," he said, absently petting the Siamese curled up in his lap. "I like cats. You know that. I love cats, and I love your cats."

"Our cats," she corrected him, softly. "They're our cats. They love you, too."

He nodded absently. "I'm sure they do. When we first met, Lucy wouldn't have curled up in anyone's lap but yours, would you girl?" He skritched the cat behind her ears, and was rewarded with a dull purr. "And now she likes sitting in Daddy's. But I can't take this any more. The house smells like cat piss, we can't have anyone over, my allergies are going berserk, and it's costing us a fortune. Every week it's another jug of that stain remover stuff, and it doesn't do any good. Thirty bucks a pop and it hasn't even dried before the damn cats are in there peeing on everything again. I can't breathe, I can't touch you without one of them jumping up on us, and I can't walk through half my damn house because we've had to turn it into a minefield to keep the cats from barfing all over themselves under the coffee table."

"It's not their fault," Jenny protested weakly. "The neighbor's cat came into the house and marked the carpet. They're just trying to take it back. For us. It's their house, too."

Sean sighed, loud and long. Startled, Lucy leapt up from his lap. With a yowl and a venom-filled backward glance, the Siamese jumped down onto the floor, then padded her way to the cat door and out. Both of them stared after her.

"I thought we were keeping that closed," Sean said mildly. "To keep the neighbor's cat from getting in and spraying the walls again. I even think it was your idea."

"I know, I know." Jenny stood and turned away from him. She hugged herself tightly and stared at the offending entrance. "I tried. But she was so miserable, and she kept yowling, and I was afraid if I kept her in here and she was unhappy that she'd start spraying because of that, and..."

"And instead the big marmalade tom got in again and peed on the bookshelves. Wonderful. Because what we really needed was a mixed bouquet of cat urine."

Sean swung himself off the couch and paced back and forth in front of the fireplace. "This has to stop. I'm sorry, I know how much you love them, but it has to stop. I can't take it any more, and we just can't afford it."

"I know," she answered, without turning to look at him. "They're good girls, Sean. They don't want to do this. With the motion sensors and the alarms in there, I promise, it'll get better."

"It's not like they've helped so far, Jenny. We've paid three thousand dollars for new carpet this year alone. It was another grand on top of that in vet bills. We give them special food and special treatment and everything short of laminating the rest of the house for their benefit, and it just doesn't work." He reached her, put a hand on her shoulder. She shuddered at his touch, but didn't pull away. "They're just pets, sweetheart. We can't live our lives around them."

"I know, I know." Jenny's voice was barely audible. She took great gulping breaths, trying not to sob. "I can get rid of them, you know. That will fix things. That'll fix everything. I'll give them away tomorrow."

Sean spun away, jerking his hand back as if it had been burned. "I don't want that. They're something that's important to you and you shouldn't have to give it up. Besides, if you do then you'll just get mad at me for making you do it, and at this point I think you like the cats more than you like me, anyway. That's just not a solution, OK?"

"But it would solve the problem."

"You'd hate me for it. I said, it's not a solution."

She turned, staring at him. "Then what do you want to do? We can't keep them locked in the bedroom.

They'll just pee all over there, even more than they do now."

"I don't know." He walked past her, into the kitchen, and took a beer out of the fridge. "I'll think of something. There are some people I can talk to about it, some friends of mine from work who are into...alternative solutions. They had an idea that I can check out. But it just can't go on like this."

"We can sell the house."

He whirled, slamming the beer down on the counter. "I am not going to be driven out of our house by your idiot cats."

"Then what do you want to do?" She stalked over to the kitchen table and stood there, fists quivering. "We can't shut them in, and we can't keep them outside, and we can't keep them from peeing on the carpet. You don't want to get rid of them, and I don't want to lock them up, and you don't want to sell the house, so I'm not really sure what options we have here."

"I don't know, all right? I just don't know. I'll think of something. I told you, I'll talk to some people." Swiping the beer off the counter, Sean took a healthy swig, then started cursing as the over-excited liquid burbled out of the mouth of the bottle. It spattered loudly on the floor, and he stood there, watching, as it overflowed.

"Well?" Jenny asked softly.

"Well, goddamn," Sean replied, his voice dangerously soft, and hurled the bottle into the sink. Somehow, miraculously, it failed to shatter, but instead spun crazily before landing, neck-down, in the disposal. Beer gurgled vociferously down the drain as Sean stood there, gaping. He glanced up at Jenny, who stood, one hand over her mouth to try to hide her laughter, then looked back into the sink, where the unbroken bottle stood as mute witness to the impotence of his rage.

"Goddamn!" he bellowed, louder this time, then turned and stomped off into the living room. One by one, the motion sensors they'd set up went off, their piercing alarms clashing with each other in ear-splitting dissonance. She heard more cursing as he yanked the front door open, and then the sound of the heavy wood slamming behind him as he went out.

Jenny took a deep breath, then walked over to the counter to grab a paper towel. She'd never seen him like this - well, not often. But he'd come back. He just needed a little time to cool off, a little time away from the cats.

Sally peered at her from behind a kitchen chair as she sopped up the beer on the floor. It wasn't that much, she saw now, surely not enough for Sean to get really upset over. A couple of quick wipes and it was all gone. She turned and tossed the soggy paper towel in the sink. It hit with a wet sound as Jenny straightened and walked away. Sally followed her, closely.

♦ "Honey."

Jenny stirred, frowning. The voice came again, soft and insistent. "Honey?"

She opened her eyes and was groggily unsurprised to discover that the room was still dark. The alarm clock on the floor told her that it was a little after three in the morning. She'd gone to bed at ten that night, still waiting for Sean to come back. The sound of the front door had awakened her an hour later, but he'd gone straight to his study instead of coming to bed. The sound of music coming down the hall told her that he was working on something—he always worked to music at home, usually loud and late at night—but after a while it turned into white noise, and she drifted off to sleep. He'd come to bed much, much later, if at all, and when she woke in the morning, he was already showered and dressed, and at work in his study.

It had been like that the next night, too, and the one after, and the one after that. Two weeks of late nights and evasive answers about a solution he was working on with those friends she never met. But he was cheerful, even hopeful instead of angry, and it seemed foolish to confront him and risk dousing the spark of hope his enthusiasm had ignited. There had been an odd smell in his study at one point, but he explained that one of the cats had brought him something furry and dead from the yard, and that he'd forgotten to take out the trash before it had gotten ripe. He'd hastened to add that he'd praised the cats for being good hunters, and really, wasn't the fact that he was happy with the cats a good thing?

Of course it was, she told herself. *It was an* important *thing*.

And now, he was there, the music off and the hallway fixture out and the dim light through the blinds showing that he was smiling. He sat on the floor next to the bed with Lucy in his lap. Sally lay at his feet, her belly exposed and eyes closed. She wasn't purring.

"Sweetheart?" She half-sat up and groped for the light.

"No, no light," he said. "Don't bother."

"Sean? What's going on?" She was awake now, a cold tightness in her gut telling her that something she didn't understand was happening here. "You're not leaving, are you?" She winced, hating herself for having asked the question. "I swear, I'll make things better."

He shook his head, but his hands still held Lucy close. "No, Jenny. I'm not leaving. I'm not going anywhere."

"Oh good, oh God, thank you." The words came out of her in a rush. "I know it's been tough with the cats and everything, and I promise I'll do everything I can to try to make them behave better and won't you behave better, girls, for Daddy? Won't you?" She stared down at the cats, lip trembling. Lucy looked back into her eyes, unblinking, unmoving.

Sean smiled. "That's not necessary, honey. I've got a solution that's going to solve all our problems."

She sat up and blinked. "You do? That's wonderful, Sean. That's amazing. Did you find something online? Tell me!"

"Something like that," he said, and snapped Lucy's neck.

"Sean, no!" The words came out in a whisper, but to her they were a ragged shriek. She wanted to reach for him, to hurl something at him, to fling herself between him and Sally so he couldn't do her any harm, but her arms refused to obey and her body sat, frozen. She watched as gently, wordlessly, he laid Lucy's body down on the carpet and took Sally in his arms. "Shh, Jenny. It's OK. It's for the best. Trust me." His hands stroked Sally's belly once, and then closed on her throat.

Her eyes obeyed her, at least. She closed them so that only the soft crack of Sally's spine told her that the deed was done. *This is it*, she told herself. *I can't stay in a house with this. I can't stay with him. I'm leaving. Oh God, what if I'm next?*

She opened her eyes, looked down at him. He sat, cross-legged and smiling, a corpse on either side of him. "It's all right, Jenny. Everything is going to be just fine.

I told you I had some friends who could help us out. That's who I went to see the other night. They're into the most interesting things, unique solutions, really, and they taught me this. I'm sorry it took so long, sweetheart, but I needed to practice. I wanted to get it right, you know."

"No, I don't know, Sean. I don't know what you're doing or why you killed our cats, but I'm leaving right now." *That's good*, she told herself. *Good, strong words. Now I just have to get up and move. But moving, doing—that had always been the problem.*

Sean put his left hand on Sally's head, his right on Lucy's. "I don't think so," he said conversationally. "I mean, you might if I gave you enough time to think about it and fret, but that would just be silly. Instead, I'm going to show you what I learned. It's going to solve all of our problems, honey. You'll have the cats but they won't do any of the things we hate, and you'll have them forever."

Her voice rose to a near-shriek. "You're going to *stuff* them?"

He laughed, softly. "No, I'm not going to stuff them. I'm going to give them back to you."

His eyes closed, and his mouth opened, and a fine mist poured out of it like water. It cascaded down, puddled in his lap and then spilled over. Tendrils of it twined around his arms and snaked around the cats, stroking them as gently as she herself had ever done. Gently, wisps of spectral smoke caressed the dead bodies' fur, slipped themselves into their mouths, and wove back and forth across their eyes.

And she watched. She watched as the last of the fog dripped from Sean's lips and his eyes opened, unseeing, as the wisps and shadows vanished into the tiny dead bodies there on the floor. She watched, and her hands tightened on the blankets. Inside, she knew, something was screaming. Something was cold and afraid and knew that things were very, very wrong, but it was buried deep down and she just sat and watched.

Under Sean's hand, Sally stirred. Rolled over. Opened her eyes, which now shone with the faintest hint of green. And started walking toward her.

She scrambled backwards, her muscles finally obeying her. "Sean? What's going on, Sean?"

"Everything is just fine, Jenny." He stood, Lucy in his arms. She swiveled her head with the faintest of grinding sounds and looked up, right into Jenny's eyes.

And purred.

"Oh, God, what have you done?" She looked away, even when a soft thump told her that Sally had jumped up on the bed, even when the cat's soft body rubbed up against her, even when the low rasp of Sally's purr let her know that she was demanding to be petted.

"They're fine, Jenny. Better than ever." Sean's voice was closer now, and she could feel the mattress shift as he sat down on the bed. "Here, take Lucy. She wants her mommy to skritch her."

Jenny shied away, her hands shoving Sally from her. The cat's fur was as soft as ever, the rumble of her purr still strong. She looked up at Jenny with hurt in her eyes, hurt and the unnatural gleam Sean had put there. "I can't do this, Sean. Take them away. Please, take them away."

"But they love you," he whispered, and put Lucy in her arms.

The weight was right. The feel was right. The purr and the tone and the texture of the fur against her skin were right. Only that soft rasp, the grinding of bone on bone, told her different. She felt the tears coming now, falling one at a time onto the thing she held in her arms. She felt her grip tighten reflexively, felt Lucy's head rub against her shoulder as she squirmed to get away from the water. The last reserves she had crumbled and she started weeping, stroking Lucy and holding her close. "I'm so sorry, girl, Mommy loves you, Mommy never wanted to hurt you, Mommy is so sorry."

"Shhh." Sean slid in beside her, wrapped his arms around her. "It's all right. Just a little pain for a moment and now they'll never hurt again."

Gently, he pushed her down to the bed, draped the cover over her. Lucy nested in her arms; Sally escaped to curl up on Sean's pillow. "We won't need to feed them any more. Won't need to clean the litter boxes. Won't have to worry about them when we go away. All of our troubles are gone, and you'll have them for the rest of our lives."

She sniffled and closed her eyes, feeling the weight of his body next to hers on the bed as he lay down beside her. "They're better off this way, honey, I promise. I love our cats. I love you."

Still weeping, she held Lucy close until felt the little body grow cold. Only then did she let the cat walk away.

◆

Richard E. Dansky was named one of the Top 20 Video Game Writers by *Gamasutra* in 2009. He is the Central Clancy Writer for Red Storm/Ubisoft and the author of the novel *Firefly Rain*, available from Gallery Books. Richard has contributed to numerous bestselling video game franchises, including *Ghost Recon, Rainbow Six,* and *Far Cry.* His most recent title is *Splinter Cell: Conviction.*

Richard lives in North Carolina with his wife, their books, and their inevitable cats. You can find him either online at http://www.richarddansky.com or in the bleachers at a Carolina Mudcats game. Take your pick.

www.richarddansky.com

"Stand Off"

by Alan Baxter

Gary wondered which one would kill him first. His terror was threatening to knock him out, his mind about to shut down. His body felt like it was nothing but a skin bag half full of cold water. His bladder had already let go. He could tell that his face was white from the cool sheen of sweat that covered him and the chill that filled him.

He sat on the filthy street, knees trembling together, feet splayed out at bizarre angles, hands somehow supporting him behind. Just as he had fallen. He could feel the cold tarmac under his hands and buttocks, the dampness seeping into the seat of his jeans, but that was probably cooling urine. He could feel tiny particles of gravel under the pads of his fingers. He was aware of all these things, but in a way that was detached, like they were somebody else's experiences. His whole body trembled with the vibration of abject terror and he stared wide eyed from one figure to the other as they stood either side of him and he wondered again which one would kill him first.

One of the figures let out a deep, rumbling chuckle. "A Mexican stand off?"

The other figure smiled broadly, his long white teeth catching any available light. "It would seem so."

They stood facing each other over Gary's supine form, staring into each other's eyes with what looked like a wary respect. Gary knew that it would be pointless to run, assuming he could move. They might not be looking at him now but he knew they would move like lightning if he so much as twitched. The one with the teeth had appeared first. The vampire. *Can I really be looking at a vampire?* It had appeared like smoke from the shadows right in front of him, teeth gleaming in the darkness. Gary had leapt back in shock and rebounded awkwardly off someone coming the other way, falling backwards between them.

And what the hell was the other one? The vampire was easy to spot, if hard to believe, but this other one was different. He had a similar build, tall and strong looking, but his face was like granite, carved and rugged. He had regular looking teeth and his skin seemed tanned. Not a look consistent with vampires. In fact, he looked entirely human but exuded an aura of immense power. There seemed to be a pale blue shimmer of light around his hands. As Gary's fear addled mind began to make these observations the vampire circled slightly to the left. The other followed suit, circling with the vampire, the two of them keeping their eyes locked and Gary, seemingly ignored, between them.

The tanned one let out another small laugh. "You seem tense."

"With reason, I think. I've heard of you."

"Really? I'm touched."

The vampire smiled again. "Hmm. You wouldn't normally spare a moment before destroying one of my kind, would you?"

The other shrugged slightly. "Don't flatter yourself."

The vampire's smile widened. It circled again to the left, the other following the movement as before. Gary began to tremble even more as the vampire disappeared from his field of view, moving behind him. His spine tingled at the thought of it no more than a few inches from his exposed back. The other one came slowly around to stand directly in front of him, looking over him as though he didn't exist.

The vampire's voice came from behind. "I just want his blood. You're welcome to whatever is left."

The tanned one shook his head. "I need him alive."

"I could drain him but not kill him."

"But he wouldn't be alive."

Gary watched the tanned one's face. His eyes were deep and black, seemingly bottomless. He had shoulder length shaggy black hair and wore a scuffed and tattered leather jacket. His jeans were worn in places, tight across muscled thighs, and he wore strong, scuffed leather boots. He moved again, circling around Gary a little more, presumably responding to the vampire's movements. The vampire appeared again in Gary's field of vision, his black jeans seemingly new, a black shirt under a heavy coat.

"So it's his soul you want?" the vampire asked.

Gary's stomach seemed to flip over, his throat tightening. *My blood or my soul?*

"What makes you think that?"

The vampire raised one eyebrow. "Isn't that what you do?"

"No. Is that really what people around here say of me?"

"In truth, most people round here don't believe you exist. But I know of you."

"And how do you know of me?"

"Let's say we have a mutual acquaintance. He speaks quite highly of you. And, as far as I know, there aren't many vampires that you wouldn't kill."

"Really? Interesting."

The vampire laughed. "Is it not true that you kill every vampire you come across? Every vampire, every lycanthrope, every witch, wizard and mage? Any creature that doesn't fit your ideal for the on-going protection of the human race?"

The other smiled. "You say human like a swear word, like it tastes bad on your tongue. Yet you would not survive without them."

"If the cows run out then the humans will eat the sheep. If it came to it then we could do the same. But there are more than enough humans to go around. They have a habit of breeding. So, am I wrong about you?"

"My agenda runs deeper than you understand. But get in my way and I won't hesitate to destroy you."

The vampire circled again. Gary's hands were beginning to go numb from the coldness of the road and the pressure of holding himself up. His eyes were wide, flicking between the two figures. He could feel his hair swimming like it was in a static field, the air between these two charged like before a storm. There was a coppery scent to the air. The large man seemed to crackle with raw energy, electric and primal. The vampire kept alert, slightly crouched, moving like a cat.

The vampire paused in front of Gary, the other one directly behind him now. "I could just rip his life from him. Are you quick enough to stop me tearing his throat out?"

"Are you quick enough to get away with it?"

The air seemed to vibrate over Gary, the tension palpable between the two.

"Convinced you could beat me in a fight, are you?" the vampire asked.

That low, rumbling laugh again. "There's absolutely no question about it."

The vampire smiled again, but the smile seemed to tremble just slightly. Gary's skin began to crawl at the thought of the one behind him. *What can scare a vampire?* It felt like he was watching a late night horror movie, only he had the mother of all front row seats. He began to wish that he had someone to pray to.

"Vincenzo says that you are the most powerful creature he has ever met," the vampire said slowly.

The was silence from behind Gary.

"Vincenzo also says that any vampire that tried to bring you down would die in seconds."

More silence. The static tension grew.

The vampire broadened his smile once more, slightly more confident. "But Vincenzo also says that you and he are allies. Vincenzo and I are…shall we say, business partners?"

"So you don't want to fight me?" The big man sounded a little disappointed.

"I'd rather not. At least, not now."

"Very sensible, I suppose. Well, I wouldn't say that we're allies, but we don't have to be enemies. Leave quietly and the fact that you exist ceases to bother me."

The vampire dipped his head in a slight bow. Slowly he stepped back, away from Gary's feet. He took a second small step, then a third. He slowly straightened up, his guard becoming more relaxed. With another nod he vanished. Quite literally disappeared. One moment Gary was staring at his handsome, pale face, then he was gone leaving nothing but a slight gust of air.

Gary sat staring into the space where the vampire had been, his trembling still making his teeth chatter gently. Slowly, he sat forward, taking the pressure off his numb palms, and brought his hands around to his lap. He began gently massaging each hand with the other.

As he sat forward he felt the dull ache of a deep bruise near his tailbone.

There was a soft grinding of boots on tarmac as the big man with the black hair walked slowly around in front of Gary. He was looking up, watching the roof of a building across the road. Gary followed his gaze and saw a silhouette on the corner of the roof, like a gargoyle in a long coat that blew in the wind. Then it was gone. The big man crouched down in front of Gary and held out his hand. "Isiah," he said.

Gary looked at the big hand, then back up at those bottomless black eyes. "What?"

"My name. Isiah."

Gary's eyes widened. "Oh, right. Sorry. Gary Blackwell." He shook Isiah's hand and tried not to jump at the weight of it. The man's hand felt like a warm rock, heavy, smooth and hard. "You, er...you just saved me from a vampire, right?"

Isiah smiled. "Yeah. You seem to be handling it pretty well."

"Well, I'm doing okay, I guess, considering. I just can't help but wonder what the hell you must be to scare off a vampire!"

Isiah's smile broadened and he nodded. "Fair point. Let's just say that I'm a good guy."

"Are you? A good guy?"

"Yeah. Kinda. Come on, let's get you up and changed."

Gary looked down at his wet jeans and felt his cheeks colour. "Yeah, not a bad idea. Sorry about that. I'm pretty embarrassed here."

Isiah shrugged. "Don't sweat it. I've seen much worse reactions than that in my time."

They didn't talk as Gary led them back to his apartment. There were a thousand things that he wanted to say, questions he wanted to ask, but it was easier to say nothing at all. It would be easiest to simply pretend all this had not happened, but his cold, wet jeans and this scary stranger beside him wouldn't allow that.

Gary's apartment was one roomed and small. There was a fold up bed, left out and unmade, a small cooker in one corner, piles of clothes all over the floor. There was a small TV on a chest of drawers in one corner, it's aerial twisted like a pretzel, with a small radio cassette player next to it and a DVD player underneath.

Isiah casually wandered the length of the room and back, checking out the books on the floor. There was no order to them, but there was a general theme; Chaos Mechanics, Quantum Theory, Space/Time. Gary was definitely fascinated by the mysteries of the physical universe. His books pointed him out to be a devout scientist, at least in a theoretical sense. There were some novels among the other books, a selection of science fiction titles from Carl Sagan's *Contact* to Star Trek and Babylon 5.

At that moment the door opened and Gary came in from the bathroom he shared with the other people on this floor. He had one towel around his waist and was using another to dry his curly brown hair. "That's better."

Isiah nodded. "You'd better get dressed again quickly. We have to go."

Gary looked up through his towel. "OK. While I was showering I had a think about what's been happening. I half expected to come back in here and find you gone and it would all turn out to be a particularly lucid dream. I fervently hoped so, in fact. However, as that hasn't happened, I need some answers."

"Fair enough." Isiah sat on the bed, then quickly stood up again. He moved the rumpled duvet aside and pulled out a laptop computer, it cables running under the covers and off the end of the bed to a phone port.

Gary reached out and took the laptop. "Sorry. Not much room in here, but it's cheap."

Isiah smiled. "Sure. Prices in the city are terrible. So, what do you want answers to? I might not be able to give you all of them."

Gary pulled on a fresh pair of jeans and started rummaging through one of his clothes piles. "Well, for one, why the hell did you and a goddamned vampire have that little game of tug o'war with me?" He pulled a t-shirt from the pile and dragged it on over his head.

Isiah leant back on his hands. "You were attacked by a vampire because you were in the wrong place at the wrong time. What were you doing wandering around there on your own anyway? You know that part of town is dangerous, don't you?"

Gary shrugged. "Sure, but I never worried too much before. I can handle myself. I mean, it's not that late, you know. And how the hell was I supposed to anticipate a vampire?"

"Well, now you know. If it's after dark then anticipate vampires. Especially in crappy areas like that.

Apparently they prefer the taste of the blood when it comes from someone bad. In fact, it wouldn't hurt to anticipate anything at all. You never know what's lurking in the dark."

"Is that right? Now I know. I'm still not sure I believe it, but I know." Gary sat on the floor and pulled on a pair of socks, then his shoes. As he reached for a pullover he said, "So you were just passing by?"

"No. Mind if I smoke?" Gary shook his head so Isiah pulled out his tobacco pouch, began to roll himself a cigarette.

"So why...? What do you...?" Gary's eyebrows raised, his expression a little lost.

Isiah licked the edge of the paper and stuck it down. He put the cigarette in his mouth and took a long drag before blowing smoke out in a thin blueish cloud. Gary stared, dumbfounded. *He didn't light it!*

"You were going to die tonight," Isiah said. "Until he appeared I wasn't sure how, but you were due to clock out. I wanted to prevent that." He shrugged.

Gary stared at him. "How did you know I was going to die? And why did you want to prevent it? Not that I'm ungrateful, you understand."

Isiah smiled thinly. "I'm privy to certain information that most people aren't. I can't really explain all the why's and how's, I'm afraid. Ideally you would never have seen me, but the vampire caught me a little off guard."

Gary sat on the floor staring at Isiah, his face showing nothing but confusion and disbelief. He started to say something, then paused, swallowing. He tried again. "So what now? You just going to wander off again, your work done?"

Isiah blew a couple of smoke rings, sent them spinning gently towards the ceiling. "No. I have to get you back to where you were going before. Where were you going before you ran into me and the vampire?"

Gary pursed his lips. "I was going to meet some friends."

Isiah nodded. "Where?"

"Duke of Gloucester."

"Right. So let's go."

Gary rubbed vigorously at his eyes with the heels of his hands. "But I was supposed to die and not get there?"

Isiah shook his head. "No. You were always supposed to get there. You dying before that was an unexpected last minute change. Ripples and echoes. I needed to prevent that. I figured it was going to be a road accident or maybe a mugging or something. So I was escorting you to the Duke of Gloucester. Then the vampire appeared and I realized what the threat was. That threat has been removed, so now you carry on with your life."

Gary's eyes widened. "As if nothing's happened?" He was rather perturbed by the matter-of-fact nature of this Isiah character. "Just go and have a few beers with my mates and pretend that I don't know that vampires really do exist and that there are people out there who never need a lighter or a box of matches!"

Isiah laughed softly. "Come on, we have to go."

Gary sat staring at Isiah a moment longer before slowly standing up. He headed towards the door, then stopped, went back and rummaged in a drawer. He saw Isiah smile as he slipped a folding knife into his pocket. Gary stared at the door for a moment, his face pale, his eyes haunted. "What's happening to me?"

Isiah took a last drag on his cigarette. As he blew out the smoke the cigarette butt vanished from his fingers. "You may well hate me by this time tomorrow, but that's the way it is for me. People will live now because you didn't die."

"How?"

Isiah stood, straightening his jacket. "Sorry, Gary, we can't really talk about this. Come on. You just have to get to the Duke of Gloucester like you'd planned to. You'd be amazed at the tiny things that can affect other people's lives. You've heard of the Butterfly Effect?"

Gary nodded. "A butterfly flaps its wings in Japan and a hurricane hits Los Angeles a month later. Chaos theory."

Isiah smiled. "Exactly. People's lives are like that. Everything you do has a million effects."

Gary looked at Isiah, apparently trying to decide if he was joking or not. "I guess I was going there anyway. In fact, I'm actually running late now." He really wasn't sure what he wanted to do. He felt like running as far from the pub and Isiah as he could, but that did not really seem like an option. If nothing else, at least he'd be able to drink when he got to the pub and drinking was a fine idea right about now. He took a deep breath. "So, I guess I'm ready."

Isiah nodded and held open the door for Gary.

As they walked down the street, Isiah looked up into the dark sky, all the stars obscured by heavy, purple clouds. There was a sheen of orange to the edges of some of the clouds. Cityglow. He was trying not to pay too much attention to Gary. It was always better if he didn't get to know people too well. Gary seemed like a pretty decent bloke. Isiah ground his teeth.

They walked through orange pools of light under each street lamp along the quiet road before turning onto the main street. The traffic whizzed by and people wandered along in each direction, ignoring each other as they passed. Gary walked with his head down, his hands stuffed deep into his jacket pockets.

After another block or so without a word passing between them Isiah paused. "Well, Gary, the pub is just around the corner."

Gary nodded. "You coming in for one?" he asked with a smile.

Isiah smiled back. "No, sorry, Gary. I'm afraid I have to move on."

Gary nodded, lips pursed. "So what do I do now?"

"Just go on into the pub, meet your friends, have a few beers. Carry on as normal."

Gary looked down at the pavement "I'm not going to pretend to understand any of what's happened today," he said quietly.

Isiah nodded. "I know."

Looking up again, Gary reached out his hand. "Still, if nothing else, thanks for saving me from a vampire!" His face was creased in disbelief still even as he spoke.

Isiah took Gary's hand and shook it. "No problem. You might want to keep it to yourself though. Even your closest friends might have trouble believing that story. Most people refuse to believe in things that they don't want to believe in, no matter how much evidence you give them."

"I guess so. I don't reckon I'd believe a story like that. And I don't have any evidence anyway."

"Exactly."

Gary took a deep breath. "I get the feeling that I won't see you again."

Isiah nodded. "Pretty unlikely. Bye, Gary."

"Yeah. See ya."

Isiah stood and watched as Gary turned away and walked towards the corner of the block.

He gently rubbed his palm, still feeling the warmth of Gary's hand. Sometimes he felt like a real bastard for the things he had to do. Maybe one day someone else would look after the Balance. As Gary neared the corner he turned and looked back. Isiah raised a hand. Gary nodded and turned the corner. Isiah dropped into the shadows and quietly followed. *Might as well see it through.*

As Gary headed across the road to the pub Isiah paused. He moved again when Gary was swallowed by the dark doorway leading into the bar. As he quickly crossed the road Isiah gathered his will, softly remoulded the structure of his face. His hair became shorter and lighter, his jaw a little squarer, his eyes changed colour and moved slightly further apart.

It was just a few subtle changes, but he appeared to be a completely different person. He took off his jacket and slung it over his arm, folded with the lining outwards so that Gary wouldn't recognise it. All his other clothes were generic enough. Gary would not spare him a second glance. He stepped into the pub and went to the corner of the bar. There was a bar stool free, up against the wall at one end. He sat on the stool and ordered a beer when the barman caught his eye.

Gary was at the bar further down, being served by a pretty young girl in tight black jeans and a t-shirt that said BITCH in big, curly letters. Gary paid his money and walked over to a table not far away where three other guys about his age were sitting. There was a general round of greetings, hand shakes and back slaps, then Gary sat down.

"We thought you weren't coming," one of them said. "We were about to leave."

Another one nodded, raising his glass. "But we'll stay now you're here, seeing as you like this place so much! Cheers, Gary!"

Gary lifted his glass and clinked it against his friends' glasses. "Cheers, lads."

Just in time. Isiah let his eye wander around the pub, searching out the others. There were a number of people, some sitting around tables like Gary and his friends, some at the bar, others just milling around. Isiah watched a group of four guys sitting around a table further from the bar. They seemed to be chatting and laughing about a book or a magazine opened out on the table in front of them. *There they are.*

At that moment the door to the pub opened and four young girls came in. They wore short skirts and tight t-shirts, high heels and too much make-up. They giggled and flapped their hands as they came in, making their way to the bar. Almost every male head in the pub turned to watch them. Isiah gently shook his head, his face a frown of disgust.

One of Gary's friends was watching the girls cross to the bar. Without taking his eyes off them he elbowed Gary in the ribs, nodding towards the girls. He said something that Isiah missed. Gary looked up and watched the girls for a moment before looking back at his friend. There was a moment of heated discussion. Gary still appeared a little shaken by his earlier encounters, but his friends and their total ignorance of the situation seemed to be calming him down. Isiah watched as the conversation grew more animated.

A couple of the guys in the other group of four seemed to be having a similar discussion.

They quickly tidied away whatever it was they had been reading and sat up straighter, glancing at each other and elbowing and punching each other between crude comments.

Isiah watched the faces of the other four sour as Gary and his friend stood up and approached the group of girls. He watched their frustration and annoyance as Gary's friend said, "Hi, girls. Why don't you let me and my friends here buy you a drink? Four of you and four of us!"

The girls giggled and fawned as the guys on the other table made angry faces and got out their book again. They got back to drinking and reading, probably talking about how those girls weren't really their type anyway. Isiah could not watch any more. The four that needed protecting were safe. He hoped they were worth it.

As he left the pub Isiah took one more glance back at Gary, now crowded around the table with his three friends and the four twisted, hellish creatures that appeared to most mortal humans as very attractive young girls. Isiah ground his teeth.

♦

Alan Baxter is an author and self-described optimistic cynic living on the beautiful south coast of NSW, Australia. He writes dark fantasy, sci fi and horror, rides a motorcycle and loves his dog.

Alan has two novels available, a number of short stories published in various places and is currently working on a third book.

You can learn all about his writing and read his blog at his website, where you'll find a lot more of his work, including a free novella. Alan also teaches Kung Fu. Feel free to tell him what you think. About anything.

Alan is the author of the dark fantasy thrillers *RealmShift* and *MageSign*. Both books are available from Gryphonwood Press.

alanbaxteronline.com

"The Death of Captain Eugene Bloodcake and the Fall of The Horrid Whore"

by Joel A. Sutherland

Although he didn't shut his trap through the entire process, Captain Eugene Bloodcake was remarkably compliant as his legs were roughly cut off from his waist.

Whinin' Butch Teach and Ham-Hands Patrick didn't see anything unusual in that; nothing unusual in a grown man being ripped apart without so much as a single grunt of discomfort. Normally, of course, they would have, but not this day. Normal no longer existed in their neck of the woods. Or their leg of the sea, as it was. Normal had gone to Hell in a hand basket the day before, when Patrick suggested that they play a game to pass the time.

"What kind o' game do ye recommend, Patrick?" Butch had asked as he absently gazed out at the horizon.

The cool blue water glistened in the fading light of the setting sun. The jagged and charred piece of wood they were floating on bobbed up and down with the sea. It was considerably tilted to the right under Patrick's girth; the combined weight of both Butch and the Captain wasn't enough to balance their makeshift barge.

Patrick hemmed, hawed and finally let his head droop. His chin tripled in the process. "I dasn't know," he said in defeat.

Butch sighed. His younger brother was idealistic, true, but everyone knew that he, Butch, the older, quicker, handsomer brother, was the idea man. He removed his ratty hat and ran a grime-covered hand through his long greasy hair. He replaced the hat to its familiar perch and smiled.

"Arrr, Patrick," he said. "I'll say somethin' I miss more than anythin', then ye'll say somethin' ye miss more than anythin'. Understand?"

Patrick nodded his round head eagerly.

"Very well. We'll start wi' drink. I miss grog."

Patrick wasted no time in replying. "I miss grog too."

"Right. How about grub? I miss roast pork."

"Me, too. I miss pork."

Butch bit the inside of his lip and wrung his hands together. "Now Patrick, how about this time ye say somethin' other than what I say? Can ye do that fer me, Patrick?"

Patrick blinked twice, which Butch took for a 'yes'.

"How about Mad Mary O'Malley?" Butch said, leaning back on his bony elbows and closing his one good eye. "She be a fine wench. She rubbed me shoulders when they ached, washed me body when 't be dirty, an' polished me cutlass when 't needed polishin', if ye catch me meanin'. Did she do any o' that fer ye, Patrick?"

Patrick smiled. "She served me grog an' pork," he said.

The Captain, who up until now had not joined in on the conversation, spoke up. "Mad Mary oft' let me wear lass' undergarments as she tickled me feet wi' a gull's feather," he said in his gruff voice without sitting up.

He was lying in between the two brothers, and had been doing so for some time.

The absurdity of his comment didn't register immediately with either Butch or Patrick, and neither answered. Instead, with a pair of yelps they both scattered from the Captain, as far away as they could get, which was only about a foot to either side.

"Like ye said, Whinin' Butch: she be a fine wench," the Captain said, apparently unaware of his mates' fear.

Patrick's wet lips quivered. "Ye spoke! But ye're, ye're, ye're-"

"Dead," Butch finished.

The Captain whipped his head to stare Butch in the eye. His bushy black beard shook in anger. "What?" he bellowed. "Dead? Don't be a bilge-suckin' blaggard! Blimey, I'm as alive as ye an' yer cowardly swab o' a laddie!"

Butch looked down upon his captain's pale bluish-grey face with an expression of dreadful apprehension. "I beg yer pardon, Cap'n Bloodcake, but durin' th' battle wi' th' French ye tookst a few hits."

The Captain grunted. "How many's a few?"

Patrick pulled the Captain's shirt up (an act which Butch believed to be a tad too bold), revealing a hairy stomach and chest, completely drained of colour, riddled with a veritable bounty of blood-crusted holes. "Seventeen," Patrick said, pointing at the evidence.

The Captain's expression turned from outrage to melancholy. "Arrr," he said.

♦ Following the revelation of that unfortunate bit of news, the Captain didn't say much for some time. He occasionally asked a one- or two-word question, and every so often he grunted or moaned in displeasure, but mostly he just stared deep into the murky sea.

Butch, who fancied himself an unrivaled storyteller, was quite content to fill his crestfallen corpse of a captain in on all the details of the battle; and Patrick, who fancied himself an unrivaled storylistener, was quite content to give ear to the events that had only recently passed.

"An' then—like a buccaneer who's been made t' kiss th' gunner's lass, flogged wi' th' cat, then scuppered overboard—th' ship sank below th' water wi' a final mighty yell, nothin' but fish food fer Davy Jones' locker."

The Captain's eyes grew moist and he discreetly wiped at them. "Th' Horrid Whore..." he whispered.

"'Fraid so, Cap'n. 'Fraid so." Butch patted Bloodcake's burly shoulder. "Our beloved ship, alas, no more."

Clear liquid snot dribbled out of Patrick's nose, over his lips and dangled from his chin. He tried to stifle a squeak of remorse, but failed.

Butch sensed that his skills were working, and ploughed ahead. "I found this piece o' wood we're floatin' on, but Patrick be the one who found ye, Cap'n. An' although ye be still kickin', ye looked as bad as a sea dog who'd danced wi' Jack Ketch, th' hangman hisself."

"I also found Hubert," Patrick added; and to prove his point, he picked Hubert, his pet rat, out of his pocket and thrust his twitching little nose right in front of the Captain's face.

Butch nodded. "This next part makes me heart wail t' report, but I feel I must."

"I died?" the Captain asked.

"Aye, ye died."

"Shiver me timbers," the Captain said.

"This mornin' we be about t' make yer body walk th' plank, as 't be, but then th' sharks appeared." Butch turned his head and pointed due south. The Captain followed his gnarly finger out to sea, where he could see three fins protruding from the water.

"An' shortly after that, yer remains began t' speak, an' that brings us all up t' speed."

"Avast, ye ought t' let me sink wi' Th' Horrid Whore; a good cap'n always goes down wi' his ship." The Captain sighed and an awkward lull descended upon the group.

Bloodcake scratched an itch on his wooden peg leg with his metal hook hand; Butch found that to be slightly unorthodox yet completely representative of his beloved captain's character.

"These sharks," the Captain said, breaking the silence. "They haven't attacked ye yet, or rammed yer raft?"

Patrick put Hubert safely back in his pocket. "Only th' baby has come near an' circled us, but th' mother an' father have always stayed aft."

With a considerable amount of squinting, the Captain could see that one of the fins was indeed a lot smaller than the other two. "Hmm," he said thoughtfully.

"Aye, Cap'n?" Butch asked.

"It's typical shark rearin' behaviour. I've seen 't a bucketful o' times before. They mean t' make a man out o' the'r lad; they mean fer th' child t' eat us."

Once again, an awkward lull descended upon them, this one far gloomier than the last. A moment later the silence was broken, not by Captain Eugene Bloodcake, but by the faint sound of the attempted suppression of a fart.

Three eyes—one live eye belonging to Butch, two dead eyes belonging to the Captain—fell upon Patrick.

Patrick blushed to his roots and grumbled, "It be Hubert."

♦ It was quarter past midnight when the baby shark decided to become a man.

For such a small creature he gave the raft a remarkably strong strike. The three pirates were jostled out of their sleep and awoke in various states of comprehension: the Captain, being a captain of the high seas for the past thirty-nine years, was the first to realize that their vessel was under attack; he attempted to jump up to his feet but, being a cadaver, was unable to move. Instead, he began to bellow. "Begad! Awake ye poxy addlepates! We be under attack by that scurvy sea dog!"

Butch rubbed his eye with the back of his hand and blinked three times. It was odd: Mad Mary O'Malley, lying beside him as naked as the day she was born, was yelling and hollering at him in Captain Bloodcake's voice. He blinked thrice more and realized his folly as his dream morphed into reality. He was on his knees at once and scrambling for a weapon.

Patrick opened his eyes for a few seconds then promptly fell back asleep.

The shark circled back around and darted straight at the raft. He hit it head-on in a spray of salt water and splintered wood; the raft threatened to overturn but narrowly stayed its course. Bloodcake continued to say things like "Avast" and "Blimey"; Butch continued his search for a weapon; and Patrick continued to snore.

Their supplies were scant; all they had managed to salvage from The Horrid Whore was some stale bread (now strikingly soggy), a seagull feather (which was of sentimental significance to the Captain), and a small coil of rope.

Th' pickin's be slim, but me time be short, Butch thought as he steeled his courage and threw caution to the wind. Without a word of warning he grabbed the rope and slapped the shark on the side of the face with it as he once again circled the raft.

The shark was not amused. When Butch cracked the rope against its face for the second time he opened his mighty jaws wide and clamped down. The rope snagged in his teeth and he yanked on the taut cord with all of his might.

Butch emitted an unintelligible word that sounded like "Eep!" and was sent flying through the air before he could let go of the rope. He hit the water with a loud smack and began to skid along its surface like a skipped stone. Luckily, the rope flew from his hands, but his head had been bashed around like a piñata; the last thing he saw before he lost consciousness was the fin of the shark; it turned around and swam straight for his submerged body. His vision went blurry then grey then black, and he sank out of sight of the raft.

Captain Bloodcake had no intention on losing one of his raftmates, especially since he assumed the rest of The Horrid Whore crew were as dead as he was (or probably even more dead), so he began to yell at the top of his lungs. It was to no avail; Patrick remained peacefully asleep. Hubert, on the other hand, peeked his beady little eyes out of Patrick's pocket. He eyed the Captain with a look that seemed to say, "What's all th' commotion about, eh?"

"Arrr, tis nay use," the Captain said in defeat. But then inspiration struck him and Bloodcake smiled at the rat. "Ye haven't eaten in a long time, have ye, me bucko? Ye must be starved. Come on then an' give a wee nibble of me good hand, here."

Hubert looked at the Captain's rotting flesh with lust, but then glanced back up at his face. "I ain't no landlubber who can be hornswaggled," he seemed to say. "Ye better not try any funny stuff, ya filthy bilge rat!"

The Captain knew Hubert was dubious of his intentions, but could see the hunger deep within his very soul written plainly on his face.

The rat darted for Bloodcake's exposed carrion.

But just as soon as he had left his pocket-home, Patrick awoke and scooped his pet up in one of his big, meaty hands. "Ah," he said. "Where do ye suppose ye be runnin' off to?" He stroked the bristly fur on Hubert's head with affection.

"Belay yer rat-pettin' ways an' dunk me in th' briny deep!" shouted the Captain.

"Yarrr?" asked Patrick.

"Whinin' Butch Teach be drownin'!"

Patrick understood immediately. He stowed Hubert safely back in his pocket, swallowed up Bloodcake's legs in his tree trunk arms and submerged him in the sea. He pushed the Captain, stiff with rigor mortis, as deep as he could; then all he could do was watch and wait as the shark rapidly approached.

Underwater, Bloodcake's motor functions were as useless as they were back on the raft. But Butch hadn't sunk completely out of reach yet. The Captain's arms, swaying slowly from side to side, dangled down below

172

his head. He willed his hook to turn so as to catch on Butch's clothes, but he couldn't move.

The shark darted in for the kill, causing turbulent water to swirl around the Captain and Butch, and as Bloodcake's hook spun it caught on Butch's vest and tore a hole in which it embedded itself.

The Captain let out an exclamation of bubbles in triumph.

Back on the raft a few seconds before this, Patrick waited nervously. In the pitch black of night it was impossible to see anything below the surface of the sea, but he didn't take his eyes off the water around the Captain's legs. The shark's fin was almost upon Bloodcake now. Patrick could only wait a few more seconds.

One…

He grit his teeth.

Two…

A great burst of air bubbles broke the surface; Patrick took that as the signal.

Three! He yanked the Captain up and out of the water, amazed at the weight of the dead man. But as he pulled Bloodcake out, he saw that he was also pulling Butch out, and that answered that.

He dropped his two nearly drowned friends onto the raft and sat back with a sigh; saving lives was hard work on an empty stomach.

Butch coughed up a lungful of water, which splattered on the deck, and then sucked in a huge breath of air. He repeated the process a few more times until he began to feel a little more like himself again, and then he lay perfectly still.

The shark circumnavigated the raft once more. Clearly upset at its missed opportunity to ascend to adulthood, it skulked back to its parents.

Patrick looked upon his brother, who he had feared he had lost. "So, we be all in one piece then?"

Butch was still shaken; he only nodded.

But Captain Bloodcake sounded remorseful. "Nay. That lily livered scum bucket plundered me good hand." If he could have he would have raised it in evidence, but as it were, Butch and Patrick had to crane their necks to witness the damage.

He was telling the truth. Where the Captain's hand should have been was nothing but air. His body had been drained of its liquids long ago from the seventeen hits the French had landed upon him, so no blood poured from his severed wrist. This simple fact amazed Butch to no end and he leaned in for a closer inspection. Amid the meaty flesh, exposed sinew and protruding wrist bone of the Captain's wound, a small white maggot emerged from the stump and wriggled in the moonlight. Butch wondered at the plausibility of that, then promptly turned his head and emptied his stomach of its final dregs of swallowed salt water.

♦ Although Butch was still visibly shaken, his ordeal with the shark provided him with fertile ground for his one true love. He was as animated as possible as he recalled the events with a slightly fandangled candour.

"Puttin' me life on th' line, I held onto th' rope wi' god-like strength; I meant t' pull th' shark in, ye see, so as t' ensnare th' beast an' feed me brother an' me cap'n a doughty feast. Unfortunately, th' sea, as we be knowin', gives no quarter, an' I began t' sink deep below."

Butch briefly considered telling Patrick and the Captain about the mermaid that pulled him back into reach of Bloodcake, but decided that particular tidbit would be more effective on land in a tavern with a mug of rum in each of his rapt listener's hands.

"An' here be th' capsheaf o' me tale: I been under th' water too long; so long, in point o' fact, that I paid a quick visit t' Jones hisself. Indeed, I saw th' bright light, th' other side, an' 't weren't till I be back on our Jollyboat, thanks t' th' valiant actions o' th' two o' ye, that I came back t' life."

Patrick whistled quietly in respect.

Bloodcake snickered; he was not easily fooled on the subject of death. "Listen gents," he said. "Now's not th' time fer talk; now's th' time fer action. We're goin' t' be out o' soggy bread soon, we still be far from land, an' them three scalawags still be givin' chase."

Sure enough, the sharks were relentless; Butch and Patrick's spirits fell when they saw the trio of fins maintaining their distance behind them.

"'Tis only a matter o' time before th' littl'un attacks us again, an' I'm fearful that when that time comes, th' Black Spot will be upon us."

Patrick swallowed audibly. "It's been nice knowin' ye'se," he said through choked tears.

"Cheer up, bucko," said Bloodcake. "We not be dead yet. Well, not ye two, anyhow. I've got a plan."

"An' what be that?" Butch asked incredulously.

A roguish smile spread across Bloodcake's face. "I've had plenty o' dealings wi' sharks in me storied life; I plan on havin' a wee parley wi' th' unfledged child."

♦ The brothers exchanged dubious looks as they held the Captain over the edge of the raft by his legs;

Butch held the flesh and bone leg while Patrick struggled to maintain his grip on the polished peg leg.

Bloodcake's face was fully submerged. Little air bubbles frequently broke the surface around his head. The shark's fin swayed from side to side as it treaded water a foot from the Captain's face. All that could be heard were muffled murmurs of the one-sided conversation.

After a few very long minutes, the shark swam away from the Captain and began circling them once again. Butch and Patrick heaved Bloodcake back up onto the raft.

"Arrr," he said once he had emptied his lungs of water, "th' shark has taken th' bait."

"But Cap'n, we have no bait t' speak of," Patrick said, nervously wringing his hands together.

"Of course we do, ye barnacle-bedecked lily cod!"

Patrick, clearly confused, looked to his brother for clarification.

Butch sighed. "He means hisself, Patrick," he said. "The Cap'n's th' bait."

"No! Not th' Cap'n," Patrick said. "Th' shark can have me lights an' liver, but not th' Cap'n!"

"I appreciate yer bravery, Patrick. But th' shark has got a taste o' me, an' it's me flesh that he now desires. But he's conceded two parts o' me body which be more valuable right now to you'se than all th' pieces o' eight in th' entire Caribbean: me legs."

Patrick threw up his hands. "I be hungry, but not that hungry! I ain't no cannibal!"

"Paddles, Patrick," Butch said. "We'll use his legs fer paddles."

"Well me hearties, time's a tickin'. Pick up me hook an' get t' th' cuttin'. Handsomely now."

As Butch and Patrick took turns sawing away at the rotting flesh holding the Captain's legs to his waist, Bloodcake composed his death chantey.

> He be a man o' salt an' sea
> An' although he only had one knee
> All buccaneers will rue th' day
> When Bloodcake wi' his life did pay
>
> Fer the French, them swabs,
> Robbed his crew o' the'r jobs
> An' sank his pride, Th' Horrid Whore
> Then sent th' Cap'n t' Jones' door
>
> But ole Bloodcake be one tough nut
> Wi' seventeen holes in his gut
> He crawled his way back t' life
> Only t' find, wi' a shark, new strife
>
> He gave his life up one more time
> T' th' shark, an' heard the death bell chime
> But his legs he gave his mates one each
> T' Ham-Hands Patrick an' Whinin' Butch Teach

Patrick, having severed the final tendon and releasing the Captain's second leg, wiped his brow of sweat and smiled. "I'm mentioned first in that chantey," he said with pride. He cleaned the bloody hook on the side of his pantaloons and put Bloodcake's arm to rest at his side. Looking to his brother he asked, "Can I be havin' th' peg leg, Butch?"

The peg leg, paddle-like in its construction, would be far easier to row with.

"We'll take turns wi' 't," Butch said.

"Tough, but fair," the Captain said. "Ye would have made an admirable first mate, Butch." He looked upon Butch and Patrick with a genuine mix of respect and affection. "Roll me o'er into th' water smartly now, lads, then weigh anchor an' be on yer merry way. An' when ye reach land, make double sure t' splice th' mainbrace fer me!"

"Aye aye, Cap'n," Butch and Patrick said in unison as they gently pushed Bloodcake's upper torso over the edge of the raft.

As he tumbled over the side, the Captain could be heard saying, "Tonight, Th' Horrid Whore an' I will sleep together again." His body hit the surface with a great splash.

Before the ripples had time to subside, the shark scooped up his booty and proudly swam back to his parents, never to bother the brothers again.

Arm in arm, Butch and Patrick watched the three shark fins, the last sign of their beloved captain, disappear in the distance. Hubert poked his head out of Patrick's pocket and squeaked solemnly.

"Godspeed," whispered Butch.

After a moment of silence, Patrick turned to his brother. "Do ye suppose I could be yer first mate?"

"That's no such thing as a first mate's first mate."

"I know."

Butch smiled and handed Patrick Captain Bloodcake's fleshy leg. "O' course ye can be me first mate."

♦ The sun was just beginning to rise above the sea in the distance, its first rays bathing them in a brilliant golden light; Butch and Patrick, legs in hand, silent silhouettes, shared a weary smile. It had been an exceptionally long night, one that would take a long time to recoup from, but they would paddle without rest for as long as it took to reach land. After all, they had grog to drink, roast pork to eat, wenches to bed, chanteys to sing, and stories to tell.

♦

Joel A. Sutherland makes his living as a librarian, surrounded by books both at work and at home. His first novel, *Frozen Blood*, was nominated for the Bram Stoker Award; Leisure Books will release an updated version in August 2011. He is also the author of *Be a Writing Superstar*, a creative writing book for kids published by Scholastic.

Sutherland recently filmed an episode of the hit television show *Wipeout* as the "Barbarian Librarian". He's happiest when he's hanging out with his wife, Colleen, his son, Charles, and their goldendoodle, Murphy. They live in Courtice, Ontario.

www.joelasutherland.com

ABOUT WILY WRITERS

Wily Writers was born on October 31st, 2008, when the private writers group was formed by Angel Leigh McCoy and Ripley Patton. On Valentine's Day, 2009, we launched (with great joy) the Wily Writers Speculative Fiction site where all the stories in this book appeared.

Wily Writers is a labor of love dedicated to helping writers build their careers, and it continues to be an amazing and fulfilling adventure. We have attracted wondrous talent to the site, also having had to reject many incredible stories. The friends of Wily Writers continue to multiply. We're blessed to have met so many great people.

Visit WilyWriters.com to find the stories in this book as audio podcasts. Drop us a line, and let us know what you think at wily@nwlink.com, or join us at Goodreads for a discussion!

ABOUT THE EDITOR

Angel Leigh McCoy is an award-winning writer herself. She has worked for game companies for many years and is currently writing for *Guild Wars 2* at ArenaNet. Horror, dark fantasy, and steampunk are her genres for fiction. She has published short stories in numerous anthologies and magazines. Visit her at AngelMcCoy.com.